INDIANA JONES
and the
LAST CRUSADE

Ryder Windham

Based on the story by George Lucas and Menno Meyjes
and the screenplay by Jeffrey Boam

LUCAS BOOKS

■ HarperCollins*Childrensbooks*

Indiana Jones and the Last Crusade
First published in Great Britain by HarperCollins Children's Books in 2008
1

978-0-00-727677-6

A CIP record for this title it available from the British Library.
77-85 Fulham Palace Road, Hammersmith, London, W6 8JB.
The HarperCollins Children's Books website is:
www.harpercollinschildrensbooks.co.uk
Printed and bound in Great Britain

Thanks to Annmarie Nye at Scholastic, and Jonathan Rinzler and Leland Chee at Lucasfilm. Thanks to Mark Cotta Vaz and Shinji Hata, authors of *From Star Wars to Indiana Jones: The Best of the Lucasfilm Archives*, which features information and numerous close-up images from Henry Jones' diary and other props. Thanks also to the authors of Lucasfilm's official Indiana Jones website (www.indianajones.com), and to Dr. David West Reynolds for his extensive knowledge about the costumes, props, and vehicles in the Indiana Jones films.

For Dorothy and Violet,
who make every day Father's Day

*I*ndiana Jones kept his horse in line with the other mounted Boy Scouts who followed their Scoutmaster, Mr. Havelock, across the red rocks of the Utah desert. It was the summer of 1912, the year that Indiana — Indy to his friends — turned thirteen. He was excited to be a member of the Boy Scouts of America, a relatively new organization, founded just a little over two years earlier.

Except for his wide-brimmed hat, Indy didn't care much for the Boy Scout uniform. And unlike his fellow scouts, he wasn't especially eager to collect merit badges, even though he had already earned five. What he liked most about being a scout was that it kept him outdoors and away from his father.

Indy and his father didn't talk much.

The Boy Scout troop proceeded past towering buttes until they arrived at the base of an ancient cliff pueblo.

Overhead, natural arches spanned like bridges across the sky. Indy marveled at the sight and tried to imagine what life must have been like for the ancestors of the Hopi, the indigenous tribe who had once made their homes at the edges and recesses of the cliffs. His admiration was such that he had adorned his Boy Scout uniform with an authentic Hopi Indian woven belt.

Mr. Havelock brought his horse to a stop, turned to the boys behind him, and cried, "Dismount!"

The boys swung off their horses. One especially hefty thirteen-year-old scout, Herman, accidentally fell from his saddle and landed hard on his side, sending his hat off of his head.

"Herman's horsesick!" teased another scout.

Indy tossed an angry glare at the teaser. He was about to step over and help Herman to his feet when he saw Herman push himself up from the ground and put his hat back on. Herman looked embarrassed. Indy caught his eye and shrugged, letting Herman know that the fall was no big deal.

Leaving their horses, the scouts followed Mr. Havelock up along the base of the cliff. "Chaps, no one wander off," Havelock said, his voice echoing off the high cliff walls. "Some of the passageways in here can run for miles."

Indy and Herman ran off on their own, scrambling up

a steep hill to investigate a pair of big, wide-mouthed caves at the top. Herman was carrying his bugle, and it glinted in the sunlight as it bounced against his hip. After Indy chose the darker of the two caves, Herman mustered up his courage and entered first. Indy followed.

As they made their way inside, the temperature dropped several degrees. They had only walked a few yards when Herman pulled up short. "I don't think this is such a good idea."

Before Indy could argue, he heard something coming from a small passage in the wall to his right. *Voices?* He stopped and gazed into it, noticing that it sloped downward. He could make out a faint light in the darkness, and caught a whiff of burning kerosene.

Herman heard the sound, too. "What is it?"

Indy knew better than to reply. He reached forward, grabbed Herman's sleeve, and tugged the larger boy after him as he stepped down into the passage. Moving quietly, they arrived at what appeared to be a large hole in the floor. But then Indy noticed the exposed wooden beams at the edges of the opening. He realized they were looking down into a *kiva*, an underground ceremonial chamber built by the ancient pueblo.

Indy and Herman hunched down and peered into the *kiva*, where several kerosene lanterns illuminated the forms of four men. Three were filthy-looking fellows, digging with shovels and pick-axes. Indy couldn't see them too well. The fourth man wore a leather waist jacket and a brown felt fedora hat, and stood with his arms crossed as he watched the others dig.

The man in the fedora was clearly in charge. "Alfred, did you get anything yet?"

"Nothing."

"Then keep digging."

Suddenly, one of the other men said, "The Kid's got something."

"Whoo! Yee-hoo!" Indy assumed the man shouting was "the Kid." He said, "I got something, Garth! I got something . . . I got something right here."

When the excited speaker turned, Indy saw he was indeed an older kid, maybe fourteen years old, with dirty blond hair. The Kid had dug up an old box, which he carried over to the man in the fedora. The other two men laid down their tools and stepped over, too. One man wore wire frame spectacles, an unbuttoned vest, and had long black hair that flowed out from under his black hat. The other man was middle-aged with a gray mustache, and was wearing a dingy old Rough Rider cavalry uniform.

Indy and Herman watched silently as Fedora — the

name that Indy had given the man below — took the box and opened it slowly. The Kid huddled close beside Fedora and said, "Oh, look at that!"

Fedora removed a bejeweled cross from the box. The cross was made of gold, as was the long, finely linked chain attached to it.

"Whoo!" the Kid shouted. "We're rich! We're rich!"

"Shut up. Shut up," muttered the long-haired man. Because of the man's spectacles, Indy thought of him as Glasses.

"Well, we're rich, ain't we?" the Kid said.

Indy removed his scout hat and bent down to get a better view of the cross. Beside him, Herman nervously whispered, "Indy . . . Indy? What are they doing?"

Indy gazed intently at the cross and hoped that his silence would encourage his companion to be quiet. It didn't work.

"Indiana?" Herman said. "Indiana?"

"Shh!" Indy responded. Herman went quiet.

Fedora blew dust off the gold cross, and then he smiled.

Glasses didn't want to waste any more time. "Hey, we got to find more stuff to bring back." While Fedora continued to examine the cross, his three allies returned to their digging.

Leaning close to Herman, Indy whispered, "It's the Cross of Coronado. Cortez gave it to him in 1520."

A moment later, the Kid found an old ring and began whooping again. "Ah! Oh, boy! Whoo!"

Looking at the ring, Glasses said, "I'm thinkin' about raisin' my dead mama, dig down, and put it on her bony finger! Ha ha!"

Indy watched Fedora place the cross upon a stone. As Fedora stepped away from the cross, Indy whispered to Herman, "That cross is an important artifact. It belongs in a museum." Rising from the edge of the *kiva*, he shifted Herman to face him and said in a low voice, "Run back and find the others. Tell Mr. Havelock that there are men looting in the caves. Have him bring the sheriff."

As Indy spoke, Herman felt something slither over his leg. A snake. His face contorted with sudden horror, but Indy casually tossed the snake aside. "It's only a snake."

Herman was still trembling, apparently too afraid to move. Indy grabbed his neckerchief and tugged it, forcing Herman to meet his eyes, and said sternly, "Did you hear what I said?"

"Right," Herman gasped. "Run back ... Mr. Havelock ... the sheriff ..." Suddenly realizing that the instructions required leaving Indy behind, Herman added, "What, what are *you* gonna do?"

Indy released the neckerchief. "I don't know," he admitted. "I'll think of something." He patted his friend on the shoulder, and Herman turned and began to make his way back up and out of the passage.

A rope dangled down from Indy's position to the floor of the *kiva*. Indy figured that the four looters had used the rope themselves, but he tested it to make sure it would hold his weight anyway. The looters continued to dig, their backs to him as he lowered himself down into the *kiva*.

Quiet as a cat, Indy slunk forward and picked up the gold cross. He nearly jumped when Fedora snapped, "Dig with your hands, not with your mouth." But Fedora was still focused on the other men and unaware of Indy's presence. Indy tucked the cross into his belt and returned to the rope. He cast a last glance back at the looters, smirking as he began to haul himself up the rope. He was just pulling himself up through the hole in the ceiling when his boots struck one of the exposed wooden beams. The beam was very brittle.

Crack!

Fedora and the others turned their heads in the direction of the sound, hardly believing what they saw: was that a Boy Scout scurrying away with the Cross of Coronado? The Kid was the first to react, exclaiming, "He's got our thing!"

"Get 'im!" Glasses yelled. Fedora grimaced as his three allies fell over each other in their haste to get their hands on the Boy Scout.

Indy removed the cross from his belt and gripped it tightly as he fled back through the passage and out of the cave. He bounded down the rocky slope that led up to the cave's entrance, kicking up dust and trying his best not to slip and break his neck. Stopping for a moment, he quickly scanned the area and shouted, "Mr. Havelock!"

No response.

"Anybody!"

Still no response. Indy couldn't see any of the other scouts and then he realized what had happened.

"Everybody's lost but me," Indy muttered.

"There he is!" shouted Fedora as he emerged from the cave above.

"Let's go! Let's go!" the other men hollered from behind.

Indy bolted, leaping from one rock to another until he arrived at the ledge that overlooked the area where he'd left his horse. He stuck two fingers into the corners of his mouth and let out a loud whistle. His obedient horse responded immediately, trotting over to stand at the base of the ledge, directly below his position. Indy slid the bejeweled cross back under his belt.

Then he jumped.

He'd intended to land squarely on the horse's saddle, and he might have succeeded if the horse hadn't stepped forward just as Indy's feet left the ledge. As gravity had it, Indy landed on the ground instead.

"Hey!" came the voice of one of the looters. "Hey you!"

Indy picked himself up and climbed onto his horse's back. "Hyah! Hyah!" The horse galloped away from the base of the ledge, just as Fedora and the others arrived.

"Hey!" the Kid hollered. "Come back here!"

Fedora put two fingers into his mouth and whistled. His whistle brought a pickup truck, which came roaring up, with an open-topped automobile right behind it. A man in an expensive white linen suit and Panama hat sat in the auto's passenger seat. Fedora and his men jumped into the back of the truck, and then the two vehicles sped off after Indy.

Indy kept his horse at a fast gallop as he raced away from the towering rock formations and into a wide, open area. Over the sound of thundering hooves, he heard the engines of the truck and car closing in.

The man in the Panama hat gestured to the looters in the truck, motioning for them to catch up with the elusive Boy Scout. "Come on!" he shouted. "Get him!"

Indy could feel his heart pounding as he crouched low

and leaned forward in his saddle. He knew his horse couldn't outrun the two vehicles, so he scanned the terrain, searching for some kind of escape route. That was when he saw a train in the distance, barreling down a railroad track.

Indy veered off, guiding his horse toward the train. The car and truck swerved after him.

"Hey!" the Kid shouted as he bounced in the back of the pickup. "Come back here!"

As he drew closer to the railroad tracks, Indy saw that he was chasing down a circus train. The train's brightly painted exterior and colorful banners proclaimed it to be the property of the Dunn & Duffy Circus, and big letters on the side of one stockcar promoted the WORLD'S TALLEST GIRAFFES; indeed, the two giraffes who extended their long necks up through open hatches in the stockcar's roof did appear to be quite tall.

At full gallop, Indy guided his horse up along the right side of the train until he reached the first box-car, right behind the coal car. Indy barely noticed the laughing clown painted on the door — all his attention was focused on the built-in ladder protruding from the side. When his horse drew level with the ladder, Indy leaned out and grabbed it. The horse veered away from the train and ran off.

As Indy scrambled up the ladder at the front of the boxcar, Glasses leaped from the pickup truck to the ladder at the rear. Indy saw him climbing up — and knew his allies were right behind. Indy took his last chance to get a running start and leaped to the roof of the stockcar carrying the giraffes. Glancing back over his shoulder, he saw Glasses in pursuit, so he ran right past the giraffes and leaped to the next car, a flatcar that carried stacks of boxes under red, white, and blue tarpaulins.

But his pursuers weren't slowing down: Rough Rider was now right behind Glasses. Indy got up, scrambled over the boxes, and then skipped over the coupling to grab the ladder on the next car. There was an open window at the front end of it, and Indy climbed right through.

Less than a minute earlier, when Indy had ridden past this stockcar on his horse, he hadn't taken any special notice of the oversized paintings of snakes or the words HOUSE OF REPTILES that adorned the stockcar's side. After all, reptiles didn't scare him. So when he entered the car at its unmarked front end, he really didn't know what he was getting himself into.

The window led Indy directly onto a wooden catwalk that stretched the length of the stockcar. The catwalk was suspended by metal bars attached to the ceiling, and the clearance was so low that Indy was forced to crawl onto it.

He had no sooner started to haul himself headfirst onto the catwalk when Glasses reached in through the window and grabbed his boots. Indy struggled to shake himself free of the man's grip, which caused the rickety catwalk to shake, too. Would it hold up? Indy couldn't be sure, and glanced briefly at what lay below him. He nearly lost his scout hat when he saw what was directly above him. It was an open pen with a straw-covered floor that contained a bunch of large crocodiles.

The crocodiles wriggled and snapped at the air. Indy gasped as he kicked free from Glasses and pulled himself forward. The catwalk began to shake more violently as the old Rough Rider scrambled in after Glasses. Below the catwalk, Indy saw open-topped bins filled with squirming snakes. He'd never seen so many snakes in his life.

The combined weight of Indy, Glasses, and Rough Rider was more than the catwalk could take. Ahead of Indy, bolts began to rip from the ceiling, and the catwalk was transformed into a sudden slide. The lower end of the catwalk fell into a water-filled vat, sending Indy careening into an uncontrollable somersault.

The water erupted in a splash as Indy's legs hit the water, and then an enormous anaconda suddenly raised its head right in front of him — and hissed. Indy's eyes went wide with fear as he pulled his legs up and rolled to his left in a desperate effort to escape the deadly snake. Unfortunately, Indy's effort cost him not only his hat, which fell away from his head, but also what was left of his nerve, for he tumbled straight into one of the adjoining vats filled with hundreds of snakes.

They were all under and over him, writhing everywhere. He felt them slither and shift against his body and through his hair and across his face. He had never imagined what it might be like to be smothered by snakes. He would have screamed if he weren't afraid to open his mouth.

With trembling hands, Indy managed to push the snakes off his face. He lifted his head and gasped out a subdued howl. He gave a louder gasp as he began pulling himself up and out of the vat, and then released an all-out scream.

Indy's scream caused Glasses and Rough Rider to recoil on the ruined catwalk, but didn't reach the ears of the engineer — the train kept moving. Trying to regain his senses, Indy saw a small rectangular clean-out door at the car's rear. He gave the door a push, and it swung on its hinges. As the train continued to rumble along the tracks, he crawled through the doorway and stepped over a coupling and onto another flatcar carrying tarp-covered supplies and tied-down crates.

Realizing that Glasses and Rough Rider weren't about to give up, he quickly turned, slammed the small door shut, and threw its locking bolt into place. And just in time, too: A moment after he stepped away from the door, the two men began hammering against it from the other side.

The Cross of Coronado was still safely tucked in Indy's belt. He had taken only a few steps toward the rear of the flatcar when he felt something wriggle against his stomach. He stopped, drove his hands down into his shirt, and frantically pulled out a long snake that had slithered into his clothes. "Oh, oh . . ." Indy gasped with disgust as he tossed the snake aside.

No sooner had the snake left Indy's fingers than the blond kid came running over the top of the reptile car. He pounced and shoved Indy against the tarp on the flatcar. Indy shoved back, launching the Kid backwards. As the Kid caught hold of the ladder at the end of the reptile car, Indy turned, jumped up onto the tarp-covered supplies, and ran to the next stockcar. The Kid recovered and ran after him.

There wasn't any door at the end of the stockcar, so Indy raced up a ladder to reach its roof. On top of some crates on the flatcar behind Indy, the Kid spotted a long wooden stick with a metal hook on one end. He grabbed the stick and lifted it fast to snag Indy's foot.

Indy tripped over the hook and fell forward onto the stockcar's roof, landing with a thud. He had no way of knowing that his landing had caused an unlit lantern to shake free and fall from the ceiling inside the stockcar. The lantern crashed against the head of the stockcar's single passenger: a large — and now very angry — rhinoceros.

Indy started to rise from the boxcar's roof, but the Kid had climbed up after him, a long knife in his left hand. Indy grabbed the Kid's left wrist and fell back against the roof with the Kid on top of him.

Indy was sprawled flat on his back, with the Kid's blade just inches from his throat. It was then that the agitated rhinoceros made his presence known by raising his head and thrusting his horn through the ceiling. The horn tore straight up through the roof, just above Indy's head.

Indy and the Kid only shifted slightly as they looked at the horn with astonishment. The horn drew back into the hole it had created, but a moment later the rhino raised his head again and tore a new hole through the roof, just beside Indy's right elbow.

Indy shot a worried glance to the face of the knife-wielding boy who straddled his chest. It was fairly obvious to him that if they didn't move immediately, the rhino might impale them. But the Kid just grinned, thinking Indy was the only one in danger, and began to lower his blade.

But his grin vanished when the rhino's horn smashed up through the roof, passing up between Indy's out-stretched legs and coming within two inches of the Kid's inner thigh. Both of them stared at the horn with stunned expressions.

"Holy smokes!" Indy said. He shoved the Kid, who tumbled to the edge of the roof but kept from falling off. As Indy rolled over and onto his knees, two gunshots issued from the end of the reptile car. Indy glanced past the Kid to see that Glasses and Rough Rider had blasted through the lock on the clean-out door. The two men scrambled out of the reptile car, eager for vengeance.

Indy got to his feet and saw a water tank alongside the track directly ahead. The tank's maneuverable water-spout extended out over the path of the moving train. Just as Glasses climbed up onto the rhino car's roof, Indy made a quick calculation and leaped for the water-spout.

Catching the spout perfectly, Indy lifted his legs and landed a solid kick against Glasses' chest. The train ran alongside as the waterspout swung a full 360 degrees around the tank, positioning Indy neatly over the roof of the last stockcar. But as Indy released his grip and landed on the stockcar's roof, he found himself face-to-face with Fedora.

Indy hadn't had a clear view of Fedora's face in the *kiva*, but was now close enough to see that the man hadn't shaved for a few days. Startled and off balance, Indy fell to his knees.

Fedora took a step toward the fallen Boy Scout. "Come on, kid. There's no way out of this."

Shifting his weight onto his hands, Indy edged away from Fedora. He backed himself straight over a hatch that was covered by thin wooden planks, too thin to support Indy. There was a loud crash as he fell through the hatch and landed on his back on the much more solid wooden floor that lay within the stockcar.

Indy felt the wind knocked out of him. There was a thin layer of straw on the floor, hardly enough to have broken his fall. He groaned as he lifted his head and sat up. His hair had fallen in front of his eyes, and when he pushed his hair back, he saw that he wasn't alone in the boxcar, and that his fellow traveler had an even thicker mane around his own head.

It was an African lion.

Seeing Indy, the lion rose slowly to his feet. Then he advanced toward Indy and growled.

Indy scrambled to his feet and backed away from the lion. The lion roared again and Indy raised his hands defensively and cried, "Hey!" Indy plastered himself against the wall. Looking for anything that he might use to defend himself, Indy saw a lion trainer's coiled whip hanging on a nail on the wall to his right.

The lion began walking toward him, its hungry eyes following the boy's every movement.

A low growl sounded as Indy reached for the whip. When he removed it from the nail, he realized it was heavier than he had anticipated. Swallowing hard, he threw his arm forward to give the whip a try. The whip unraveled awkwardly, and its tip flew back and hit him in the face, cutting his chin.

Indy's head jerked back at the sudden, stinging pain. With his free hand, he reached up to feel the already bleeding gash below his lower lip. Then the lion roared again — the wound would have to wait.

Holding his arm out and trying to get a better feel for the whip, Indy lashed out again. The whip cracked sharply. The lion bellowed and swatted at the air. Indy didn't want to strike the lion, only drive it back, so he took a cautious step forward and snapped the whip again. There was another loud crack, and the lion began to back away.

The Cross of Coronado had slipped from Indy's belt and lay at the center of the floor. As the lion backed up against the far end of the stockcar, Indy held the whip tight with one hand as he reached down with the other to pluck up the cross and return it to his belt.

Indy had every reason to assume the lion car's doors were locked from the outside. He wondered, *How do I get out of here?*

"Toss up the whip," a voice said from above.

Indy glanced up to see Fedora's head leaning over the ceiling's open hatch. Glasses and Rough Rider were also hunkered around the hatch. Fedora extended his right arm down toward Indy.

Indy tossed one end of the whip up to Fedora and coiled the other end around his arm. Just then, the lion advanced toward Indy. Indy gasped as the lion sprang at him but held tight to the whip. As Fedora pulled him up, Indy felt the lion's front paws brush against his legs. But it was too late — he was already being lifted through the hatch and onto the boxcar's roof.

Standing atop the boxcar, Indy faced the four looters. Rough Rider drew his revolver and aimed it at Indy, but Fedora grabbed the revolver's barrel and forced it down.

Fedora's eyes flicked to the cross at Indy's belt. With some admiration in his voice, Fedora said, "You got heart, kid, but that belongs to me."

"It belongs to Coronado," Indy said defiantly as he pulled the cross from his belt, holding it out and away from the men.

"Coronado is dead," Fedora replied sharply, "and so are all of his grandchildren."

"This should be in a museum," Indy said sternly.

Tired of the conversation, the Kid lunged for Indy. "Now give it back!"

Suddenly, Glasses moved behind Indy and grabbed his arms while the Kid tried to tear the cross from Indy's grip. Indy didn't let go, even when he felt something shift inside his shirt. It was another snake. But this time, Indy didn't squirm. He stayed perfectly still, letting it exit his sleeve and wrap around the Kid's hand.

"A snake!" the Kid hollered as he released his grasp on the cross. "Snake! Aah!"

Indy twisted out from Glasses' clutches and clambered down the end of the lion car, taking the cross with him. He touched down outside the front door to the caboose. Hoping he wasn't about to walk in on another deadly animal, Indy glanced at the letters painted above the door: DR. FANTASY'S MAGIC CABOOSE.

"Magic?" Indy said aloud as he pondered his next move. Knowing that the looters would soon be on top of him, he threw the door open and entered the car.

Back atop the lion car, Fedora put his arm out, gesturing to the others not to follow the Boy Scout. "Hold it," Fedora said. "Make sure he doesn't double back."

The caboose's interior was lined by large boxes and assorted equipment for a magic show. At the far end, there was a door with a barred window, where he could see the tracks recede behind the train. But when he tugged at the door's handle, he found it was securely locked.

Indy realized the men would enter the caboose in seconds. Glancing around, he noticed a large, ornately painted wooden box that appeared big enough to conceal him. He stepped quickly over to the box, lifted its upper lid, and discovered that the box was empty. With the cross once again tucked inside his belt, Indy climbed into the box and lowered the lid.

Fedora threw the caboose's front door open just in time to see the large box's lid settle in place. Closing the door behind him, Fedora stepped toward the box.

"Okay, kid," Fedora said as Indy's weight shifted inside the box, causing it to shake. "Out of the box. Now!"

Incredibly, the shaking box suddenly collapsed, with all four sides flopping away from its rectangular wooden base to reveal nothing but empty air. Fedora gaped, but his amazement gave way to anger, and he cursed as he ran to the back of the caboose.

The door's lock didn't inconvenience Fedora a bit. It snapped as he yanked the door open, and then he stepped out onto the caboose's balcony. He saw the Boy Scout running alongside the tracks and away from the train. Fedora cursed under his breath, but as he watched the scout running off with the cross, he couldn't help but smile. He really did admire the kid's spirit.

Indy ran all the way to the town where he lived with his father. Clutching the Cross of Coronado, he glanced back over his shoulder more than once to make sure that none of the looters were following him. He ran past the industrial brick buildings that bordered the railroad tracks and headed up a street that was lined by modest houses, most with clapboard siding. Although Indy and his father had only lived in Utah for a short time, the sun had already done a solid job of fading the painted white letters that spelled *Jones* on the wooden mailbox outside of their small house.

"Dad!" Indy shouted as he neared the house. He bolted past the mailbox and up the dirt path that led to his front porch. The house had a sun-bleached stucco exterior with green trim, and the surrounding lawn hadn't been mowed since long before he and his father moved in. Usually, the sight of the run-down house or the prospect of any conversation with his father made Indy feel depressed, but right now, he only felt elated.

"Dad!" Indy shouted again as he flung open the front door and carried the cross into the house. "Dad!"

Indy's dog, a big Alaskan malamute, was lying on the floor in the front room, just outside the door that led to Indy's father's study. The dog raised his head and barked as Indy skipped past him and threw open the door. The study was filled with books, and its windows overlooked the cruddy backyard. As usual, Indy's father was seated at his desk beside a window, with a large, open book laid out before him. He was using a pen to copy an image from the book into his own notebook.

"Dad!"

"Out," the elder Jones responded without looking up, causing Indy to stop in his tracks. His father had a deep, commanding voice, and people usually listened to it.

Ignoring his father's order, Indy thrust his arm out to display the Cross of Coronado and said, "It's important!"

"Then wait," his father said, his eyes never straying from his work. "Count to twenty."

"No, Dad," Indy said defiantly. "You *listen* to me —"

"Junior!" his father snapped, clearly outraged. Still, he did not turn his gaze to Indy.

Indy hated it when his father called him *Junior*. Every time he heard it, he felt infuriated and — even worse —

deflated. Hoping his father would eventually look his way, Indy began counting out loud: "One, two, three, four . . ."

Without turning his head, Indy's father raised his left index finger and said, "In Greek."

Indy's father was Professor Henry Jones, formerly of Princeton University and an expert on medieval chivalric code. The book he happened to be examining at the moment was a medieval-era parchment volume, which was opened to an illuminated picture that resembled a design for a stained-glass window; the design incorporated an armored knight and a series of Roman numerals. Henry Jones had recently begun work at Four Corners University in Las Mesas, which was why he and Indy had moved to Utah. Indy couldn't stand his father's habit of transforming every attempt at conversation into an educational exercise. His father had become only more insufferable over the past few months, ever since Indy's mother died.

Indy wanted desperately for his father to look up and see the Cross of Coronado. He also wanted his father to see his rumpled Boy Scout uniform and the dirt on his face and the gash on his chin that was still bleeding. Indy wanted to tell his father all about what had happened that day, but he couldn't even get the man to look away from his old book. And so Indy did as he was told, and began counting to twenty in Greek.

"Ena, dyo, tria . . ."

Just then, a bugle sounded from outside. Indy glanced out a side window to see an automobile pulling up outside his house. The town sheriff and another man were in the front seat. In the back seat, Herman held his trumpet high and blew for all he was worth, proud that he had delivered the cavalry to Indy's home.

"Tessera," Indy continued counting as he moved for the study's door. Glancing at his preoccupied father, he added, "Pente," and then exited the study, quietly closing the door behind him.

Henry Jones remained so engrossed by his work that he didn't notice Indy's departure. As he continued copying the image of the knight into his notebook, he said to himself, "May he who illuminated this . . . illuminate me."

Outside the study, Indy was halfway across the front room when the front door opened and Herman walked in, proudly blowing his bugle. Indy reached for the horn, pulling it out of Herman's mouth, which was a mistake. Herman wasn't done blowing and accidentally spat right into his face. Indy flinched.

Herman was so excited and pleased he could hardly contain himself. Smiling broadly, he pointed to the door and blubbered, "I brought the sheriff!"

The sheriff walked in, followed by the man he'd been riding with in the car. The sheriff wore a big brown hat that matched the color of his caterpillar-like mustache, but his hat's height did nothing to disguise the fact that he was several inches shorter than Indy.

"Just the man I want to see," Indy said, stepping up to look down into the sheriff's eyes. "Now, there were five or six of them —"

"It's all right, son," the sheriff said calmly.

"They came after me —"

"You still got it?" the sheriff interrupted.

Realizing the sheriff meant the Cross of Coronado, Indy smiled and said, "Well, yes, sir." He held the cross up for the sheriff's inspection and said, "It's right here."

"I'm glad to see that," the sheriff said as he took the cross from Indy, "because the rightful owner of this cross won't press charges if you give it back. He's got witnesses. Five or six of them."

The front door opened again, and Fedora, Glasses, Rough Rider, and the Kid walked right into Indy's house. The looters just stood there, staring at Indy. Unlike the other men, including the sheriff and his partner, Fedora showed some degree of courtesy by removing his hat, and then he nodded at Indy in a friendly manner.

The sheriff and Fedora are in cahoots?! Indy couldn't believe it. He felt suddenly ill and his jaw went slack.

The sheriff turned his head to look through a window. Indy followed his gaze and saw another automobile had pulled up outside his house. It was the car that carried the man in the white linen suit and the Panama hat. The man had an obnoxiously large red flower in the lapel of his jacket, and used a cane as he stepped away from the car.

The sheriff handed the Cross of Coronado to Fedora, who in turn handed it back to the Kid. He took the cross and cried, "Whoo! Yeah!" as he carried it through the door and out of the house.

Indy was speechless. His mouth twitched, and the dull pain that came with it made him realize his chin would probably need stitches. He looked through the window again, and this time he saw the Kid hand the cross over to the man with the Panama Hat. The man took the cross, examining it for a moment. Then he reached into his jacket pocket and removed a large packet, which he handed to the Kid.

Money, Indy thought with disgust. *They dug up the cross for some dirty money!* He shifted his gaze to Fedora, then his eyes flicked to the sheriff. The sheriff tilted his head to Indy and said, "Good day," and then turned on his heel to walk out of the house.

The other men followed the sheriff, but Fedora lingered for a moment, long enough to face Indy and say, "You lost today, kid, but it doesn't mean you have to like it."

Before Indy could think of a response, Fedora took his hat and placed it squarely on top of Indy's head. And that's how Fedora left Indy, standing in the dingy, book-filled house in Utah, his head adorned by a rumpled, well-worn brown fedora that was slightly too large for him.

Fedora couldn't tell what the future held, but he knew that the kid would eventually grow into that hat.

CHAPTER ONE

*I*ndiana Jones's hat kept some of the rain off his face, but it didn't do anything to stop the fist that slammed into his face — not that he had expected it to. The year was 1938, and among the many things he'd learned since he'd first acquired his fedora was that a hat didn't offer much protection in a fistfight, especially when one's arms were pinned behind one's back.

Indy was standing on a cargo ship, which was currently being tossed around in a storm somewhere off the coast of Portugal. His arms were held by two sailors while a third — the one who had just punched him — stood before him on the ship's rain-drenched deck. As Indy felt blood flowing from the corner of his mouth, he lifted his head and bared his teeth in a broad, defiant smile.

The sailor hit him again.

The waves pounded against the ship and Indy braced himself for another punch, but then another figure emerged onto the deck. Indy hadn't seen the man in twenty-six years, and even though they'd both aged, there was no mistaking the man he remembered as Panama Hat. He still wore a white linen suit with a red flower in his lapel and still walked with a cane. When he left the bridge and began limping down a flight of metal steps to the slick deck, the sailor who'd been hitting Indy stepped aside while the other two tightened their grip on his arms.

Moving carefully but steadily across the deck, Panama Hat limped straight up to Indy. Because he preferred dry climates and indoor saloons and routinely hired other people to do his dirty work, Indy was surprised to see the man venture onto the deck without so much as a servant carrying an umbrella by his side. When the man was close enough for Indy to smell the liquor on his breath, he came to a stop and said, "Small world, Doctor Jones."

"Too small for two of us," Indy said boldly.

As rain pounded down on them, the man pushed Indy's leather jacket aside to expose the shoulder bag that rested against Indy's hip. Panama Hat dipped his tobacco-stained fingers into the bag and removed the Cross of Coronado. Raising his gaze to Indy, he said, "This is the second time I've had to reclaim my property from you."

Indy said, "That belongs in a museum."

"So do you." He glared at the two sailors who held Indy's arms and said, "Throw him over the side." Panama Hat began moving back toward the bridge, following the sailor who'd been using Indy's head as a punching bag, and taking the cross with him.

The two sailors held tight to Indy as they maneuvered him across the deck toward the rail. Another sailor stood at the rail, and he flung open a metal gate that was normally used to access the gangplank. But there wasn't any gangplank now — just a sheer drop into the cold, stormy sea.

A thirty-foot wave crashed against the side of the ship. Held fast by the two sailors, Indy lifted his legs and kicked out at the sailor who'd opened the gate. The sailor screamed as the kick knocked him past the gate and off of the ship.

On the other side of the deck, Panama Hat heard the scream and assumed it had been Indy's. He grinned. He was so eager to get back inside the bridge and out of his soaking-wet suit, he didn't bother to glance back in Indy's direction.

Another wave blasted over Indy and his captors. One of the sailors stumbled. Indy shoved him aside, then drove his elbow into the other sailor and flipped him to the deck. Turning fast, Indy sighted his next target heading back up the steps to the bridge.

As rain and waves continued to hammer the ship, Indy scrambled past a stack of fuel drums and over to the metal steps that led up to the bridge. He tackled Panama Hat and yanked him from the steps. The man howled in pain as he landed hard on the deck. Indy grabbed the Cross of Coronado.

But no sooner had Indy reclaimed the cross than two sailors jumped him. The cross was knocked from his grasp and skidded across the deck. A fire hose was coiled on a wall mount beside the nearby steps, and Indy grabbed the hose's metal nozzle. Using the nozzle like a club, he struck his attackers, knocking them both to the deck.

As another wave swept over the ship, it struck the fallen cross and carried it to the edge of the deck. Indy leaped away from the men and snatched the cross a split second before the rushing water would have sent it into the sea.

The ship tilted sharply, sending several fuel drums sliding across the deck. Indy scrambled to his feet and dodged the sliding drums as he moved fast for the stern, where a tarpaulin covered a high stack of wooden crates.

Panama Hat recovered and began pulling himself up the steps to the bridge. Gripping a rail as he turned to see Indy running off with the cross, he shouted, "Grab him! He's getting away! Stop him!"

The sailors came at Indy. He pummeled two of them with a single punch. Turning fast, Indy saw part of the tarp slip away from the crates.

The crates were marked TNT — MUITO EXPLO-SIVO.

Glancing up, Indy saw a large stevedore's hook swinging above the crates. He quickly climbed up onto the crates, grabbed the hook, and then leaped away. He swung out over the deck, narrowly avoiding a huge wave just as it smashed into the side of the ship, and then released the hook. He fell well past the ship's port rail and plunged into the rollicking ocean, never losing his grip on the cross.

On the ship, yet another wave struck a fuel drum and sent it flying straight onto a crate of TNT. The crate exploded, causing the entire ship to blow. Indy ducked down below the water's surface as the explosion sent an enormous orange fireball into the sky.

Cinders were still falling through the air when Indy bobbed up in the water amidst the debris. Clutching the cross, he reached out his arms, desperately trying to snag some piece of debris that might keep him afloat. He could hardly believe his eyes when he saw one of the ship's life preservers drifting nearby.

Indy looped his arm through the preserver. As he clung to it, he saw the destroyed ship begin to sink into the sea.

The last he saw of it was the painted letters on the stern that spelled out the ship's name: CORONADO.

A moment later, a shredded Panama hat floated past him. *Good riddance*, Indy thought. His own waterlogged hat had somehow remained on his head throughout the ordeal.

When Indy caught his breath, he began to kick his legs. It was a long way back to shore, and there was no time to waste.

CHAPTER TWO

*I*t was a balmy day in Fairfield, New York, and Indiana Jones — known as Dr. Jones to his students — was back at Barnett College, where he'd been teaching archaeology since he'd transferred from Marshall College in Connecticut.

Indy stood before the blackboard in his classroom, wearing a clean shave, British-made spectacles, a tweed suit, and a bow tie. Most of his students, who watched him attentively from their rows of tiered desks, would never have guessed that their well-groomed teacher was a rugged adventurer and the sole survivor of a recent shipwreck off the Portuguese coast. Facing the blackboard, Indy said, "Archaeology is the search for *fact* . . ." He used a piece of chalk to write the word FACT for emphasis, then turned his gaze to his students and added, ". . . not truth. If it's truth you're interested in, Dr. Tyree's philosophy class is right down the hall."

Indy's students chuckled at this. When the laughter subsided, most of the female students went back to staring at their handsome professor. Staying focused on his lecture, Indy continued, "So forget any ideas you've got about lost cities, exotic travel, and digging up the world. We do not follow maps to buried treasure, and 'X' never, *ever* marks the spot."

In the corridor outside Indy's classroom, his friend and patron, Marcus Brody, Curator for the National Museum of New York, approached the room's door. Brody was wearing a gray suit with a dark striped tie. When he reached the door, he peered through its window to see Indy before he reached for the doorknob.

"Seventy percent of all archaeology is done in the library," Indy said. "Research. Reading." Indy saw the door open and Brody stepped in. While Brody walked over to stand against a wall beside the first row of tiered desks, Indy continued, "We cannot afford to take mythology at face value."

The bell rang. As the students began filing past his desk and out of the room, Indy announced, "Next week: 'Egyptology.' Starting with the excavation of Naukratis by Flinders Petrie in 1885. I will be in my office, if anybody's got any problems, for the next hour and a half."

After the last student had left, Brody walked over

to Indy. Indy leaned on his desk and said, "Marcus. I did it."

"You've got it?!" Brody said excitedly.

Indy reached into a desk drawer and removed a green cloth bag. He placed the bag on his desk. Brody opened it and gazed upon the Cross of Coronado.

"Oh!" Marcus gasped as he picked up the cross.

Removing his glasses, Indy said, "You know how long I've been looking for that?"

"All your life," Brody said, his eyes riveted to the cross.

"All my life," Indy said. He pocketed his glasses.

"Well done, Indy," Marcus praised. "Very well done indeed. This will find a place of honor in our Spanish collection."

Indy picked up a stack of books and tucked them under his left arm. Turning for the door, he said, "We can discuss my honorarium over dinner and champagne tonight." Before he walked out, he aimed a finger at Brody and added, "Your treat."

"Yes," Marcus said as he continued to admire the cross. "My treat." He remained absorbed by the cross as he followed Indy out of the classroom.

Indy headed for his office, where he anticipated a few students would want to meet with him. But as he opened the door to the reception area outside his office, he was momentarily speechless to find dozens — possibly *all* of his students — crammed into the room. Seeing him, the students began calling out his name trying to get his undivided attention.

"Dr. Jones!" cried a student. "Dr. Jones!"

While some students shouted and held notebooks out for Indy to examine, the few female students who were nearest to him just tilted their heads back to gaze up at him with mute, adoring expressions. The reception room hadn't been designed to accommodate such a crowd, and Indy felt the temperature rise more than a few degrees.

"Shush!" he said to the demanding students. "Shush! Shush!"

"Dr. Jones!" called out another female voice. Indy almost shushed her, too, before he saw the speaker was his secretary, an overwhelmed teaching assistant named Irene. "I am so glad you're back," Irene said frantically. She was holding a stack of papers which she handed to Indy in batches. "Here are your phone messages. This is your appointment schedule, and these term papers *still* haven't been graded."

"Okay," Indy said as he began jostling past the students, who became more desperate and vocal as he neared his office door. "Irene, put everyone's name on a list, in the order they arrived, and I'll see each and every one of them . . . *in turn*!"

The students were still clamoring for Indy's attention as he entered his office and shut the door behind him. The door had a frosted glass window, which was supposed to allow the passage of some light as well as maintain privacy, but right now, all it did was display the shadows of the students' outstretched, waving hands. Indy felt as if he were suffocating.

Indy's cramped office was on the ground floor in Hamilton Hall, but given that he shared the space with a large boiler, it may as well have been in the basement. The room's walls were lined with deep shelves loaded with ancient artifacts, most of which Indy had picked up on his travels.

As he sat in the chair behind his desk and set his books and paperwork aside, his eyes flicked to his fedora, which rested on his cluttered desktop. Seeing the hat gave him a pang, a reminder of his life outside the walls of the college. Then his eyes fell on another object on his desk, a small package that was wrapped in brown paper and bound with twine. Inspecting the postmark, he read aloud, "'Venice, Italy.'"

The students began banging their hands against his door.

Indy took one last look at the door. Then grabbed his hat, opened the window, and climbed through it, stepping onto the green lawn outside Hamilton Hall. He shoved the package from Italy into one of his jacket pockets and then began walking away from the building with a brisk, determined stride.

Indy saw some students and faculty milling about outside. Hoping to appear innocuous, he stuck both hands in his pockets and kept his head down as he walked up along the green beside Grove Avenue, practically whistling with relief.

The sun was out. There was a breeze in the air. Indy felt better with every step he took away from the college buildings.

He didn't see the long black Packard sedan that was parked outside Hamilton Hall and was unaware that the sedan's passengers had seen his window exit. He hadn't walked far when the sedan moved off from its parking spot, trailing him just a short distance before a man called from the moving vehicle, "Dr. Jones!"

Indy stopped. So did the car. Three men got out. One of them said, "Dr. Jones?"

Indy kept his hands in his pockets as he eyed the three men. They were all stocky fellows with no-nonsense expressions, and there was nothing flashy about their suits, hats, or shoes. Everything about the men suggested that they were government agents, the kind of men who could be most persuasive when they asked someone to take a ride with them.

Indy didn't like the way the three men had interrupted his escape from Hamilton Hall, but they didn't intimidate him either. The way he figured it, a ride with them would probably prove more interesting than the pile of paperwork waiting back at his office.

He got into their car.

Indy was delivered to a luxury apartment building in New York City, where his caretakers ushered him into a private elevator that carried him up to the penthouse. The next thing Indy knew, the three men were gone, and he was standing alone in a surprisingly large, airy reception room that was elegantly furnished and free of clutter. Tall windows offered sweeping views of the skyline and Central Park. Along one curved bay of windows, a semi-circle of plush white lounge chairs were arranged below a wide skylight. The skylight housed a contemporary crystal chandelier that resembled nothing less than an incredibly expensive arrangement of icicle stalactites. From beyond a set of double doors, Indy heard muffled conversation and music playing in an adjoining room. It sounded like a cocktail party.

Throughout the reception room, streamlined shelves and built-in niches displayed museum-quality artifacts. Indy took the opportunity to examine some of the ancient objects, but he kept his hat on. Although he was curious about the identity of the apartment's owner, he hadn't *asked* to be brought to New York City and didn't feel any need to be polite.

An ivory figure of a recumbent bull caught Indy's eye. At a glance, he pegged it as an Assyrian piece from the ninth or eighth century B.C. The bull's head was turned sharply to its left, and one of its horns was partly missing, but it was still a good find. *You don't see one of those in someone's home every day*, he thought.

Just then, the double doors swung open to reveal a silver-haired man wearing a black tuxedo. The man had the broad shoulders and trim physique of a young man, but Indy guessed he was probably in his late fifties. As the man pulled the doors closed behind him, he smiled gently at Indy and said, "I trust your trip down was comfortable, Dr. Jones. Uh, my men didn't alarm you, I hope." Crossing the room and extending his right hand to Indy, the man said, "My name is Donovan. Walter Donovan."

Donovan had phrased his name as if it were a question. Indy took the man's hand and shook it. "I know who you are, Mr. Donovan," Indy said. Then Indy, deciding to show some courtesy, removed his hat as he added, "Your contributions to the museum over the years have been extremely generous."

Donovan gave a gratified nod.

Letting his gaze sweep across the room, Indy said, "Some of the pieces in your collection are very impressive."

Donovan beamed. "Well, like yourself, Dr. Jones, I have a *passion* for antiquities." Motioning with his hand for Indy to follow, he stepped over to a circular-topped marble table and said, "Have a look over here." There was a cloth-covered object on the table. As Donovan pulled back the cloth to reveal the object, he said, "This might interest you."

The object was a fragment of a flat stone tablet, which originally might have been about two feet square. The fragment was dominated by the lower half of a symbol of a cross, which was surrounded by engraved text.

Indy placed his hat beside the tablet, removed his glasses from his pocket, and put them on. Leaning over to inspect the tablet more closely, he said, "Well, it's sandstone. Christian symbol. Early Latin text. Mid-twelfth century, I should think."

Indy raised his gaze to Donovan. Donovan said, "That was our assessment as well."

Returning his gaze to the tablet, Indy said, "Where did this come from?"

"My engineers unearthed it in the mountain region north of Ankara while excavating for copper," Donovan said. There was a slight twinkle in his eye when he added, "Can you translate the inscription?"

Translating inscriptions was no easy matter, even for someone as knowledgeable as Indy. He moved his finger along the edge of the tablet as he read aloud, "'... who drinks the water I shall give him, says the Lord, will have a ... spring inside him welling up for ... eternal life.'"

Eternal life? Indy had his doubts about the authenticity of such words, and he raised his eyebrows and chuckled under his breath. While Donovan stepped over to another table and poured champagne into two fluted glasses that rested on a silver tray, Indy resumed his translation. "'Let them bring me to your holy mountain in the place where you dwell. Across the desert and through the mountain to the Canyon of the Crescent Moon, to the temple where the cup that —'"

Donovan held a glass of champagne in each hand, and he smiled as Indy raised his gaze to meet Donovan's. Indy wore a slightly stunned expression as he recited the remaining text: "'Where the cup that holds the blood of Jesus Christ resides forever.'"

"The Holy Grail, Dr. Jones," Donovan said as he carried the glasses over to Indy. "The chalice used by Christ during the Last Supper. The cup that caught His blood at the crucifixion and was entrusted to Joseph of Arimathaea."

"The Arthur legend," Indy said as he accepted a glass. "I've heard this bedtime story before."

"*Eternal life*, Dr. Jones!" Donovan said brightly. "The gift of youth to whoever drinks from the Grail. Oh, now *that's* a bedtime story I'd like to wake up to!"

"An old man's dream," Indy said as he raised his glass to take a sip.

"Every man's dream," Donovan insisted. "Including your father's, I believe."

The mere mention of his father made Indy go tense, and he nearly choked on the champagne. Regaining his composure, he lowered his glass and said, "Grail lore is his hobby. He's a teacher of medieval literature. The one the students hope they don't *get*."

Just then, the double doors opened again. Indy and Donovan turned to see Donovan's wife, a matronly woman in a black evening gown and a gold necklace. Some other well-dressed people were visible in the room behind her. Smiling sweetly, she said, "Walter, you're neglecting your guests."

"Be along in a moment, dear," Donovan said, stepping over to his wife to kiss her cheek. She looked in Indy's direction, but he had already returned his attention to the stone tablet and had his back to her. Mrs. Donovan left the reception room, closing the doors behind her.

Indy had set his champagne beside the stone tablet.

He dipped his finger into the champagne, and then rubbed his moistened finger over a small area of the tablet's surface to remove a thin layer of dirt. Donovan returned to Indy's side and said, "Hard to resist, isn't it? The Holy Grail's final resting place described in detail!"

"What good is it?" Indy said. "This Grail tablet speaks of deserts and mountains and canyons. Pretty vague. Where do you want to start looking? Maybe if the tablet were intact, you'd have something to go on, but the entire top portion is missing."

"Just the same," Donovan said, "an attempt to recover the Grail is currently underway."

Currently underway? Indy looked at Donovan with a bemused expression. If Donovan had already begun searching for the Grail, Indy had to assume that the man lacked judgment.

But Donovan was very serious. He said, "Let me tell you another 'bedtime story,' Dr. Jones. After the Grail was entrusted to Joseph of Arimathaea, it disappeared, and was lost for a thousand years before it was found again by three knights of the First Crusade. Three brothers, to be exact."

Indy grinned. *That old chestnut*, he thought, *and Donovan actually buys it*. Figuring he'd humor the mil-
᾿ ᾳire just to see what happened, Indy said, "I've heard as well. Two of these brothers walked out of the

desert one hundred and fifty years after having found the Grail and began the long journey back to France, but only one of them made it. And before dying of *extreme* old age, he supposedly imparted his tale to . . ." Indy tried for a moment to remember the story, and suddenly recalled, "to a Franciscan Friar, I think."

"Not 'supposedly,' Dr. Jones," Donovan said with conviction. He gestured to an ancient leather-bound volume that was set on a curved shelf that hugged the wall. The volume was opened to display Latin text on two illuminated pages that appeared very brittle. Donovan continued, "This is the manuscript in which the friar chronicled the knight's story. It doesn't reveal the location of the Grail, I'm afraid, but the knight promised that two markers that had been left behind *would*."

While Indy studied the displayed pages, Donovan walked back over to the table that supported the stone tablet. Donovan said, "This tablet is one of those markers. It proves the knight's story is true. But as you pointed out . . . it's incomplete. Now, the second marker is entombed with the knight's dead brother. Our project leader believes that tomb to be located within the city of Venice, Italy."

Venice, Italy? Indy had been thinking of Venice recently, maybe even earlier that day, but he couldn't remember just when or why. He looked at the tablet and then back at the ancient volume. Donovan had obviously gone to some effort to gather his information, and Indy wondered if the man might be on to something. Not the Grail, necessarily, but *something*. While Indy carefully turned the volume's right page to examine the preceding spread, Donovan said, "As you can now see, Dr. Jones, we're about to complete a great quest that began almost two thousand years ago. We're only one step away."

"That's usually when the ground falls out from underneath your feet," Indy said, casting a cautionary glance at Donovan.

"You could be more right than you know," Donovan said mysteriously.

"Yes?"

"We've hit a snag," Donovan said, his brow furrowing. "Our project leader has vanished, along with all his research. We received a cable from his colleague, Dr. Schneider, who has no idea of his whereabouts or what's become of him. I want you to pick up the trail where he left off. Find the man, and you will find the Grail."

Indy grinned again. "You've got the wrong Jones, Mr. Donovan," he said as he crossed the room and picked up his hat from the table. "Why don't you try my father?"

"We already have," Donovan said. "Your father is the ·who has disappeared."

CHAPTER THREE

Your father and I have been friends since time began," Marcus Brody said as he climbed out of the Ford coupe that Indy had parked in the driveway outside a white clapboard house. "I've watched you grow up, Indy," Marcus continued as he followed him from the car and onto the short path that led to the front porch. "I've watched the two of you grow apart. I've never seen you this concerned about him before."

Indy found the front door open. "Dad?" he called out quietly as he walked through the doorway and into the dark hall. Glancing back at Brody, he responded, "He's an academic. A bookworm. He's not a field man." Then Indy called out again. "Dad? Dad?"

Faded green curtains hung over a wide doorway, separating the hall from the sitting room. Indy and Brody reached up to push the curtains aside and found that the sitting room had been ransacked.

Bookshelves and tables had been overturned, and books and papers were lying all over the floor. There was a fireplace on the far side of the room, and the two electric sconces above the mantle had been left on, as had the overhead light and the lamp on the desk to Indy's left. A fan whirred away on the desk, and all of the desk's drawers had been opened and emptied. Beyond the desk, French doors had been thrown open to expose the house's small kitchen. The kitchen lights had been left on too, and the refrigerator door was hanging wide open.

"Dear God," Brody said as Indy stepped into the sitting room. "What has the old fool got himself into now?"

"I don't know," Indy said as he surveyed the damage, "but whatever it is, he's in way over his head." He stepped across the scattered papers, threw open the door to another room, and shouted, "Dad?"

No response. Indy looked back at Brody, who had found a stack of postmarked envelopes that rested on the desk. Brody's brow wrinkled as he picked up the envelopes. "It's today's mail," he said, "and it's been opened."

Indy's mind reeled. *Dad's missing, and someone tears up everything in his house, including today's mail.* Suddenly it hit him. "Mail," he said. "That's it, Marcus." He reached into his jacket pocket and removed the brown paper package he had found earlier that day, on his own desk at

Hamilton Hall. Turning the package over in his hands, he looked at the postmark again and said, "Venice, Italy."

Indy grimaced. During his conversation with Walter Donovan, he had thought Donovan's mention of Venice sounded familiar. According to Donovan, Indy's father had been last seen in Venice, searching for a tomb that somehow served as the second marker to the location of the Holy Grail.

Indy tore open the package and removed a small book. It was covered in brown cow leather. Indy recognized it at once.

"What is it?" Brody asked.

"It's Dad's Grail diary," Indy said as he opened the book and began flipping through the pages. Nearly every page was filled with detailed notations and sketches, all written and drawn by Indy's father. "Every clue he ever followed," Indy said. "Every discovery he made. A complete record of his search for the Holy Grail. This is his whole life. Why would he have sent this to me?"

"I don't know," Brody said, "but someone must want it pretty badly."

Clutching his father's diary, Indy stumbled over to the fireplace. Above the mantle hung a small medieval painting, a depiction of Christ on the cross. Positioned below Christ was the figure of a woman, Ecclesia, who represented the Church, and who sat upon a beast composed of a winged man, a lion, a bull, and an eagle, which represented the Gospel writers, Matthew, Mark, Luke, and John. Blood flowed from Christ's wounds, and Ecclesia captured the blood in a chalice.

Indy turned to Brody and asked, "Do you believe, Marcus?"

Before Brody could reply, Indy noticed a second painting on another wall, to the left of the French doors. The second painting depicted eleventh century knights plummeting to their deaths over a high cliff. One knight, however, appeared to float safely in midair as he "walked" toward the hovering Grail. Turning away from the painting to face Brody, Indy asked, "Do you believe the Grail actually exists?"

"The search for the Cup of Christ is the search for the divine in all of us," Brody said. "But if you want facts, Indy, I've none to give you. At my age, I'm prepared to take a few things on faith."

Indy looked down at his father's desk and was surprised to see his father's face staring back at him. The photo had been taken years ago, when Indy was still a kid, and it showed his father as a dark-haired man, with a thick beard and a mustache that only intensified his brooding features. Some papers were partially covering the photo, and Indy pushed them aside to reveal the image of an unsmiling boy standing beside Henry Jones. The boy was gazing at something to his left, away from Henry Jones and the lens of the camera, and looked like he'd rather be anywhere else than having his picture taken beside that man.

The boy had been Indy. The photograph had been taken when his mother was still alive.

Indy left the photo on the desk but felt his grip tighten on his father's diary. He looked to Brody and said, "Call Donovan, Marcus. Tell him I'll take that ticket to Venice now." Indy headed for the front door.

"I'll tell him we'll take two," Brody said.

A private, twin-engine airliner, adorned with Walter Donovan's corporate logo, waited for Indy and Brody at the airport in New York. They arrived at the airport with Donovan in his limousine. While the airliner's engines revved, the limo's chauffer opened the door and Brody climbed out, but then stopped and turned to face Donovan, who remained on the backseat.

"All right," Brody said anxiously, "tell me what's going to happen when we get to Venice."

"Don't worry," Donovan said with assurance. "Dr. Schneider will be there to meet you."

"Uh, Schneider?" Brody said.

"I maintain an apartment in Venice," Donovan said. "It's at your disposal."

"Oh, well," Brody muttered, "that's good. Thank you." He shook Donovan's hand and then stepped away from the limo.

Indy had been sitting beside Donovan, waiting for Brody to move out of the way so he could climb out, too. As he moved past Donovan, Donovan said, "Dr. Jones . . . good luck." They shook hands, and Donovan added earnestly, "Now, be very careful. Don't trust *anybody*."

Indy nodded and then walked away from the limo. He had never been convinced that the Grail actually existed. Still, there was the matter of finding his father. If Donovan was willing to finance the trip to Venice, Indy was glad to let him pay for it.

Without a word, Indy and Brody boarded the airliner.

The flight from New York to Venice required stops in Newfoundland, the Azores, and Portugal. Indy spent much of the time studying his father's Grail diary. Henry Jones had notes on everything from ancient legends and medieval poetry to the histories of knights and battles, all related to the existence of the Holy Grail. There were also detailed maps, including one of a place called the "mountain road," and sketches of various obstacles that one might encounter before finding the Grail. Henry Jones had even speculated on the spiritual properties of the Grail.

One two-page spread was illustrated with an ink sketch of a detail from a stained-glass window, which showed a knight holding a shield that had a cross on it. The cross's lower half resembled the design of the partial cross on the Grail tablet fragment Indy had seen in Donovan's apartment. Henry Jones had also indicated that the Roman numerals III, VII, and X seemed to have some significance in relation to the stained-glass window or the knight, but Indy couldn't figure the purpose of the numbers, or how they were supposed to add up. A statue of a lion that supported an "upper floor" was also illustrated, and another spread showed a series of sculpted lions perched atop stone columns. The diary also contained a few pieces of folded parchment, including a rubbing of the Grail tablet fragment — a full-size copy of the words and partial cross — no doubt made by Henry Jones himself.

The diary was hardly easy to read, which didn't surprise Indy one bit. No one had ever claimed that Henry Jones was an easy man to understand.

Venice, on the other hand, was something that Indy understood perfectly. He'd visited the city before, and found much to admire about the old architecture, the vast network of canals and countless bridges, and the gondolas that carried passengers from place to place. As Indy and Brody disembarked a water bus onto a boat landing across the canal from Piazza San Marco, Indy sighed and said, "Ah, Venice ..."

"Yes," Brody said distractedly from under his black bowler hat.

Indy was wearing his fedora. Both men wore pale gray suits, and were followed off the water taxi by a young Italian boy who carried their luggage. While Indy soaked in the sights around him, Brody was focused on more practical matters. "How will we recognize this Dr. Schneider when we see him?"

"I don't know," Indy said as he led Brody and their luggage carrier down a gangplank from the dock to the sidewalk. "Maybe he'll know us."

Just then, from behind Indy and Brody, a woman's voice said, "Dr. Jones?"

Indy, Brody, and the young boy turned to see a woman standing near the end of the gangplank. She wore a dark gray suit and skirt that complimented her long blonde hair.

"Yes?" Indy was surprised he hadn't noticed her when he'd been walking down the gangplank.

"I knew it was you," the woman said with a smile. "You have your father's eyes."

"And my mother's ears," Indy said with brazen charm, "but the rest belongs to you."

The woman smirked and said, "Looks like the best parts have already been spoken for."

Indy thought her accent was Austrian, but he wasn't sure. As he grinned at her, she looked past his shoulder to the man behind him and said, "Marcus Brody?"

"That's right," Brody said, removing his hat.

"Dr. Elsa Schneider," the woman said as she extended her hand to Brody.

"Oh, how do you do?" Brody said, shaking her hand.

Like Brody, Indy had assumed Dr. Schneider would be a man. Indy didn't always like surprises, but this one wasn't so bad.

CHAPTER FOUR

As things turned out, Dr. Elsa Schneider also had a room at Walter Donovan's spacious apartment in Venice. After paying their young porter and leaving their luggage at the apartment, Indy and Brody walked with Elsa along a narrow canal that was lined with buildings on either side. Indy liked the way Elsa walked, like a healthy athlete with a good sense of direction.

"The last time I saw your father," Elsa said to Indy, "we were in the library. He was very close to tracking down the knight's tomb." Then she laughed brightly and added, "I've never seen him so excited. He was as giddy as a schoolboy."

"Who? Attila the Professor?" Indy said. "He was never giddy, even when he was a schoolboy."

They were walking past a street vendor who was selling flowers as they approached a small footbridge that spanned the canal. As Elsa turned to step up onto the bridge, Indy deftly reached out and stole a single flower from the vendor. Brody witnessed Indy's action with some astonishment and glanced back at the oblivious vendor as he followed Elsa and Indy onto the bridge.

Catching up with Elsa on the middle of the bridge, Indy held the flower out to her and said, "*Fräulein,* will you permit me?"

"I usually don't," Elsa said, not breaking her stride.

"I usually don't, either," Indy said.

"In that case, I permit you."

"It would make me very happy," Indy said, and he inserted the flower into the lapel of her jacket as they descended the other side of the bridge.

"But I'm already sad," Elsa said as they headed away from the bridge. "By tomorrow, it will have faded."

"Tomorrow," Indy said, "I'll steal you another."

"I hate to interrupt you," Brody broke in with irritation, "but the reason we're here —"

"Yes," Elsa said. "I have something to show you." Reaching into her jacket pocket, she removed a slip of paper and handed it to Indy. "I left your father working in the library. He sent me to the map section to fetch an ancient plan of the city. When I got back to his table, he'd gone, with all his papers except for that scrap, which I found near his chair."

Indy looked at the scrap, and then held it up for Brody to see. "Roman numerals."

"Here is the library," Elsa said as she led the two men toward a large building that loomed over a wide piazza where people walked about and sat at tables. The building was made of white marble, and its façade had tall columns with ornate capitals. Most of its windows had been bricked over, and there were two empty niches on either side of the arched main doorway.

"That doesn't look much like a library," Indy said.

Brody noticed the empty niches, which had probably once held statues, and added, "Looks like a converted church."

Elsa led the men into the building. "In this case it's the literal truth," she said. "We are on holy ground." Their heels clacked across the marble floor as they passed silent patrons and aisles lined by tall bookshelves, and proceeded into a chamber with a high ceiling. Elsa walked toward a wall that housed a stained-glass window with two massive marble columns on each side of the window. "These columns over here," Elsa added, "were brought back as spoils of war after the sacking of Byzantium during the Crusades."

The stained-glass window depicted several religious figures, and at its center was a knight carrying a shield. Below the window, several brass stands held red cordons to prevent the general public from getting too close to the wall or glass. When Elsa arrived at the cordons, she stopped and turned to Indy and Brody. "Now, please excuse me," she said. "The library's closing in a few moments. I'll arrange for us to stay a little longer."

Elsa walked off, taking the sound of her clacking heels with her, but Indy didn't watch her go. He had noticed the sculpted lions on top of the columns, and now his eyes were riveted on the stained-glass window. Lowering his voice to almost a whisper, Indy said, "Marcus . . . I've seen this window before."

"Where?"

"Right here, in Dad's diary." Indy removed the book from his pocket. Flipping through the pages, he found the two pages he had studied during the flight to Venice. Holding Henry Jones' illustration of the window up for Brody's inspection, he said, "You see?"

Indy and Brody lifted their gaze to the window. "Look, Indy," Brody said. "The Roman numerals."

Indeed, the three Roman numerals that Henry Jones had written on a scrap of paper had been worked into the window's design, set within scrolls that were positioned beneath the central knight and two female figures. "Dad was onto something here."

"Well, now we know the source of the numbers," Brody said, "but we still don't know what they mean."

An increasingly loud clacking sound announced Elsa's approach. Taking advantage of their last few moments alone, Indy faced Brody and spoke gravely. "Dad sent me this diary for a reason. Until we find out why, I suggest we keep it to ourselves." Indy returned the diary to his pocket.

"Find something?" Elsa asked as she drew up beside the men.

"Uh, yes," Brody said, directing Elsa's attention to the stained glass. "Three, seven, and ten. That window seems to be the source of the Roman numerals."

Gazing at the window, Elsa gasped, "My God, I must be blind."

"Dad wasn't looking for a book about the knight's tomb," Indy said, "he was looking for the tomb itself!" Looking from Marcus to Elsa, he continued, "Don't you get it? The tomb is somewhere in the library! You said yourself it used to be a church. Look."

Stepping to the right of the window, Indy directed their gaze to one of the marble columns, on which had been carved *III*.

"Three," Indy said, pointing to the numerals. He looked to the window and pointed to the lower left corner, where a yellow-glass scroll contained three I-shaped strips of lead. "Three," Indy said again.

Then Indy pointed to an engraved column on the left, where he found an engraved *VII*. "Seven," he said, and then quickly redirected his index finger to the window, where the same numerals were set within the glass scroll below the shield-bearing knight. "Seven."

At the bottom right of the window, there was a glass scroll with an *X* in it. "Ten." Indy reached into his pocket to pull out the scrap of paper that Elsa had given him. Seeing the *X* on the paper, Indy said, "And ten." He let his gaze travel to the surrounding walls and bookshelves. "Now where's the ten? Look around for the ten."

While Brody and Elsa stepped away from the cordoned area to inspect the nearby aisles, Indy walked over to inspect the bookshelves on the wall opposite the window, but quickly dismissed them. *These shelves were built for the library, not the church.* He glanced at a wrought iron spiral staircase that traveled to the library's upper level, but figured that the staircase was installed at the same time as the shelves.

The ten is probably set in stone. Clutching the scrap of paper with the Roman numerals on it, he returned his attention to the window and the columns.

"Three and seven," he muttered as he paced beside the cordons. *Could the numerals be a code?* "Seven and seven . . . and ten." Indy froze. He had let his gaze fall from the columns, window, and walls, and was now looking at the floor. He stared at the floor's center, walking backwards to get a better view.

Remembering the staircase, Indy ran over to it and up the steps. When he reached the catwalk on the upper level, Indy gazed down at Elsa and Brody, who had moved back to the center of the room. The floor beneath their feet was an elaborate tile design that contained a huge *X* that was only clearly discernible from Indy's elevated vantage point.

"Ten," Indy said as he pointed to the floor. Then he shrugged and added wryly, "X marks the spot."

Indy rushed down the staircase and went to the center tile where the two sides of the *X* intersected. While Brody and Elsa watched, he knelt on the floor and bent over to blow dust out of from the narrow gap that separated the tile from those that surrounded it. Unfortunately, the exposed gap wasn't wide enough for his fingers to grip the tile's edges.

Eager to see what was beneath the tile, and hopeful that he was on the right trail to find his missing father, Indy jumped up and ran over to one of the brass stands that held the cordon below the stained-glass window. After removing the cordon from the brass stand, he carried the stand back to the central tile.

Indy glanced around to make sure only Brody and Elsa were watching. He gripped the upper part of the stand as if it were the handle of a sledgehammer, and then he lifted the stand and swung, bringing its metal base down hard on the edge of the tile.

Elsewhere in the library, at the same moment that the stand struck the tile, an elderly, bespectacled librarian with wavy white hair brought a stamp down upon the back page of a book that lay open beside a stack of books on his desk. The librarian had been stamping books on a daily basis for many years, and this was the first time his action seemed to produce a loud thud that echoed throughout the building. Unaware that an unauthorized archaeological dig was going on in a nearby room, he pressed his stamp on an inkpad before bringing it down on the page of another book. Again, there was a loud thud, and he wondered if something had perhaps finally gone wrong with his hearing. When he stamped a third book and heard yet another thud, he looked at the stamp warily. Then he placed it gingerly on top of the book stack, deciding that perhaps he'd had enough for the day.

Indy didn't know that his three strikes at the floor had coincidentally caused a librarian to seriously question his own ears and contemplate retirement. But he could clearly see that his handiwork had shattered the edge of the tile, leaving a hole that he could get his hand into. Setting the brass stand aside, he bent down to lift the tile up and out of the floor, leaving a two-foot square hole at the center of the *X*.

While Brody hung back a short distance, Elsa knelt beside Indy. Cold air and a wet, rancid smell escaped from the hole. Indy said, "Bingo."

"You don't disappoint, Dr. Jones," Elsa said. "You're a great deal like your father."

"Except *he's* lost, and I'm not." Indy knew Elsa had meant to compliment him, but he didn't like being compared with his father at all.

"Lower me down," Elsa said, swinging her long legs into the hole and raising her arms to Indy.

Indy was impressed and cooperated agreeably. He gripped her wrists and lowered her into the opening. When her feet had safely reached the ground below, he released his grip and stood up beside Brody. He retrieved his father's Grail diary from his pocket and handed it to his friend. "Look after this for me, will you?"

Indy didn't tell Brody, but he'd kept one item from his father's diary in his pocket: the rubbing that his father had made of the Grail tablet, which Indy thought might come in handy. Brody tucked the diary into his own pocket while Indy crouched down and lowered himself through the hole.

When Indy touched down in the subterranean chamber beside Elsa, he was even more impressed with her.

They had arrived in a dank, dark place, and the floor was littered with human skulls and other skeletal fragments. Numerous holes had been carved out of the surrounding walls, and nearly every one contained a leering skull. Plunging into such a horrid, foul-smelling environment would have made most people tremble or even scream, but from the slight smile on Elsa's face, Indy realized she was as eager to explore the place as he was.

There was a steep step just below them. Indy jumped down, and then turned to look up at Elsa and said, "Come on." He helped her down, and they moved away from the step.

Elsa removed a cigarette lighter from her pocket and lit it to illuminate some markings that were carved into a wall. "Pagan symbols," she observed. "Fourth or fifth century."

"Right," Indy said. "Six hundred years before the Crusades." He glanced at the flickering light and noticed that the lighter Elsa held had a four-leaf clover design on it. Then he looked to his left, where shadows indicated the mouth of a dark passageway.

Lifting her gaze to Indy, Elsa said, "The Christians would have dug their own passages and burial chambers centuries later."

"That's right," Indy said, taking the lighter from Elsa. "If there's a Knight of the First Crusade entombed down here, that's where we'll find him." Holding the lighter out in front of him, Indy reached out with his free hand to take Elsa's, and then guided her into the passage.

While Indy and Elsa ventured deeper into the catacombs, Brody remained stationed in the library room. He knelt beside the rectangular hole in the floor, patiently waiting for Indy and Elsa to return. He never heard the three men who made their way down the spiral staircase behind him.

The three men had dark hair and similar mustaches. Identical dark gray suits, silk neckties, and red fezzes only furthered their mutual resemblance. And each one carried a pistol.

One of the men moved silently up behind Brody. The man raised his gun and brought it down hard on the back of Brody's head. Brody gasped, collapsing unconscious beside the hole.

Brody's assailant made a sweeping gesture with his gun toward Brody's body. The man's two accomplices grabbed Brody's wrists and dragged him away from the hole and into one of the book-lined aisles.

CHAPTER FIVE

*I*ndiana Jones and Elsa Schneider proceeded through the catacombs. Indy held tight to Elsa's lighter as they walked past the decomposing corpses that rested in niches carved into the stone walls, the grotesque skeletal remains with rotting linen stretched across blackened bones. It wasn't until they rounded a dark corner that Indy saw something that made him stop in his tracks.

It was a faded-gold relief, partially covered by cobwebs, which had been carved into the wall. Elsa followed Indy's gaze and leaned closer to the relief to brush away the cobwebs. Gazing at the remains of the image, she said, "What's this one?"

"The Ark of the Covenant," Indy answered tersely.

Elsa's brow wrinkled. "Are you sure?"

"Pretty sure," Indy said. Not seeing any need to go into details, he raised the lighter and moved on. Elsa followed.

They entered another passage. At the end, a wall of

rough stone was almost completely obscured by cobwebs. Indy ran his hand over the stones and felt a slight breeze. He began brushing away the cobwebs, revealing small gaps and cracks between the stones. On one stone, someone had carved the Roman numeral X.

"Watch out," Indy said, handing the lighter back to Elsa. Indy took a step back and then rammed his shoulder into the wall. Several stones loosened. Indy struck the wall again, this time with so much force that it collapsed on impact, sending him tumbling into the next chamber.

Indy fell onto a group of rocks that were surrounded by a bubbling, slimy liquid. Curious, Indy dipped his hand into it and rubbed his fingers together. Then he looked back at the hole in the wall behind him, where Elsa stood holding her lighter.

"Petroleum," Indy said, wincing at the smell. "I could sink a well down here and retire." He pushed himself up to his feet. His suit was filthy.

Indy noticed some cloth-covered skeletons in a nearby niche at the edge of the bubbling pool. He reached down and pulled out a strip of cloth and a length of bone, and then quickly fashioned a crude torch. After dipping the cloth end into the oil-slick water, he turned to Elsa. "Give me the lighter."

Elsa handed the lighter to Indy, and he lit the torch. He held it high above the wet floor as they continued their journey into the catacombs. Although they'd tried to stay on the rocks, they soon found themselves wading through ankle-deep water. But that wasn't the worst of it. As they ducked through an arched stone doorway to enter a narrow passage, Indy looked down and said, "Oh, rats."

Elsa gasped.

The place was teeming with rats. Thousands of them. There wasn't enough room for the rodents to move across the stones, so they crawled on one another's backs and thrashed in the water. They were all squealing and squirming.

Indy knew it was best to keep moving. He kicked his legs forward through the rat-infested water. Elsa let out a small scream as the rats darted over her feet. Indy stumbled slightly, and Elsa gasped again as more rats scampered around her.

Indy got his footing and turned to Elsa. He could see she was terrified, and he didn't blame her in the least. "Come on," he said. Holding the torch in his right hand, he leaned over, scooping Elsa up in a fluid motion. He draped her body over his left shoulder and carried her out of the chamber and into the next passage.

The three men who had subdued Marcus Brody did not linger in the library. Carrying flashlights as well as their pistols, they followed Indy and Elsa down into the catacombs.

The men were familiar with the underground passages, and they noticed every sign of trespass. When they saw the rocky debris below the hole that Indy had formed in the crumbling wall and the scattered human bones that rested amidst the bubbling oil-slick water, they knew they were still on the right trail.

Indy had hoped there would be fewer rats in the next passage, but there weren't. Fortunately, Elsa quickly regained her composure and insisted that Indy didn't have to carry her any longer.

The floor of the passage now resembled a long, deep brook of black, briny water. Narrow ledges lined both walls, and the rats scampered along them in a steady stream. Indy climbed up onto one ledge and Elsa took the other. They moved slowly on the opposite ledges, trying not to disturb the rats that squirmed in the crevices at their sides, while stepping over and sometimes on the rats that darted around their ankles.

Indy was wondering whether they were still on the right path to the tomb when the passage's two ledges terminated on either side of an arched doorway. Still holding his torch, he lowered himself into the knee-deep stream of water. He looked back over his shoulder and beckoned Elsa to join him. "Come here."

Elsa placed a hand on Indy's shoulder and stepped down into the water. She followed him through the arched doorway and into a large burial chamber. There were several ancient coffins in the room, some jutting above the water, and others resting in niches. The coffins were made of ornately carved oak, fairly well preserved despite some obvious water damage. Human skulls decorated the chamber's walls.

Surveying the coffins, Indy said, "Look, it . . . it must be one of these."

Elsa waded forward into the chamber. As she moved past the coffins, she gazed at them with admiration. "Look at the artistry of these carvings and the scrollwork."

At the end of the chamber, a single coffin was elevated on a high niche that kept it above the others and out of the water. The coffin's carved sides depicted a group of knights. Steps led up to the coffin, and Elsa climbed them to examine the coffin more closely. Beaming, she proclaimed, "It's this one."

Indy held the torch high as he climbed up beside Elsa. After Elsa blew some dust off the coffin's lid, they gripped the lower edge of the lid and shoved it back. Within the coffin lay the decomposed remains of a knight in armor. The skeletal arms still grasped a sword and shield that rested upon the lower half of the knight's body. A fine layer of dust covered the shield's surface.

"This is it," Indy gasped. "We found it!" Handing the torch to Elsa, he climbed up over the coffin to position himself above the shield. "Look," he said, and then he bent down to blow the dust from the shield, revealing detailed engravings of a large cruciform surrounded by Latin text. "The engraving on the shield, it's the same as on the Grail tablet! The shield is the second marker!"

Indy removed the folded parchment in his pocket. As he began to rapidly unfold the parchment, Elsa looked at it and asked, "What's that?"

"It's a rubbing Dad made of the Grail tablet," Indy answered as he smoothed the parchment over the shield and aligned the two designs. The engravings on the lower half of the shield matched the parchment's rubbing perfectly, and the upper half contained all the text that was missing from Donovan's tablet fragment. Indy retrieved a small drawing stick from his pocket and dragged it back and forth over the parchment. A broad, excited smile creased his face as his action extended the rubbing to include the entire shield.

Seeing how excited Indy was by their discovery, Elsa said, "Just like your father — giddy as a schoolboy. Wouldn't it be wonderful if he were here now to see this?"

Indy chuckled. "He never would have made it past the rats!" he said as he continued to rub the parchment. "He hates rats. He's scared to death of them."

Back at the hole in the wall where Indy had assembled his bone-fragment torch, the man who had knocked out Marcus Brody struck a wooden match along the side of a matchbox. The man smiled at the thought of what he was about to do and then tossed the flaming match onto the oil-slick water.

Indy had just completed his rubbing and was folding up the parchment when he and Elsa heard what sounded like a distant, muffled explosion. Then the noise grew louder, like an incoming roar, accompanied by the panicked shrieks of thousands of rats. A moment later, the rats came stampeding around the corner of the narrow passageway and into the burial chamber.

Indy scrambled down from the coffin and shoved the folded parchment into his pocket. As Elsa gripped the torch and gazed back to the burial chamber's entrance, Indy shouted, "Get back! Back against the wall!"

Elsa stepped away from Indy and placed the torch in a

dry niche while he bent down and shoved the entire coffin over, spilling the remains of the knight into the water below. The overturned coffin bobbed in the water. "Quick! Under it!" Indy shouted. "Air pocket!" As the words left his mouth, a wave of fire blasted into the chamber.

Indy shoved Elsa down under the water then ducked under himself. A moment later, flames filled the chamber and transformed it into a massive oven.

Keeping their bodies submerged, Indy and Elsa gasped as they raised their heads into the air pocket formed within the inverted coffin. Elsa was still catching her breath when Indy said, "Don't wander off."

"What?" Elsa said, turning to Indy as he took a deep inhale. "What?!" she repeated louder and more anxiously, but Indy had already ducked back under the water.

Holding his breath, Indy searched the chamber's lower walls for an escape route. The chamber's walls were brightly illuminated by the inferno from above. The oily water stung Indy's eyes, but he kept them open until he saw what looked like a dark area.

Another passage!

Moving fast, Indy rose back under the inverted coffin. He'd only been gone for a few seconds, but when his head surfaced beside Elsa's, her face was filled with terror.

Rats, desperate to escape the flames, had begun to force their way into the coffin. The ones that didn't swim in from below tore their way through charred and splintered wood. Some had landed on Elsa's head and shoulders.

"I think I've found a way out!" Indy said as he brushed a rat from Elsa's hair. "Deep breath!"

They both took deep breaths, and then dived under the water again. Indy held tight to Elsa's hand and hauled her after him as he swam toward the dark area he'd spotted earlier. It was a broken section of wall. They passed through it and up a long water-filled tunnel. Lungs straining, they saw a faint light above them before they broke the surface.

Indy and Elsa had emerged at the bottom of a storm drain. The light from above was daylight, streaming down in shafts through a circular iron grate. A metal ladder was built into the wall of the shaft. Indy started climbing. Elsa followed.

Pigeons had settled around the top of the iron grate. The pigeons hopped and fluttered away as Indy pushed up against the grate and shoved it aside. He was soaking wet from head to toe as he climbed out of the shaft. As he rose to a standing position beside the open shaft, he bumped a table behind him, and then looked around to see that he had emerged in the middle of the crowded café in the piazza outside the converted library. Well-dressed café customers recoiled at the sight and smell of Indy.

Indy let his gaze sweep over the piazza. Smiling wryly, he said, "Ah, Venice."

Looking down, he saw Elsa coming up the shaft, and he reached down to help her out. Like Indy, her hair and clothes were drenched and stank of petroleum.

There was another loud flurry of pigeons, this time from the entrance to the library. Indy glanced toward the entrance and saw six men wearing gray suits and red fezzes come running out. One of the men sighted Indy and then gestured to the others to run toward the café.

Indy had never seen them before, but he had a hunch that the fire in the catacombs hadn't been an accident. As the six men ran toward him and Elsa, he saw that one had done a lousy job of using a jacket to conceal what appeared to be a machine gun. Indy grabbed Elsa's hand and tugged her after him as he bolted from the astonished café customers.

Hoping to elude their mysterious pursuers, Indy and Elsa fled the piazza and ran down an alley between two old brick buildings. The alley ended at a rocky jetty, where three men were seated and playing a card game in a dry-docked gondola. Three open-topped wooden motorboats were moored in the water beside the pier.

Indy and Elsa ran to one of the motorboats. They released the boat's mooring lines and jumped into the front cockpit. As Indy slid behind the steering wheel and gunned the engine, the three nearby cardplayers looked up from their game in surprise. Elsa glanced back and saw the Turkish men come hurtling out of the alley and onto the jetty.

Indy launched the boat forward, but as it pulled away, one of the men leaped from the jetty and landed on the back of the boat. Both Indy and Elsa heard a *thud* at the man's impact. While Indy accelerated and weaved through the water in an effort to shake off his uninvited passenger, the other five pursuers scrambled into the two remaining boats. The three cardplayers were too stunned to protest.

Indy's boat had a loud, powerful engine. He had it going full speed, racing past some large barges along an industrial pier, when he turned and leaped from the cockpit. Elsa grabbed the steering wheel as Indy flung himself at the man who'd jumped onto the boat's stern. He had hoped to shove the man off, but a moment later, they were engaged in a wrestling match on the back of the boat, and Indy's opponent drew an automatic pistol.

Indy grabbed the man's wrist and tried to angle the gun's barrel away from his body as he fell back against the boat. The man threw his weight on top of Indy, pinning him. But Indy held tight to the man's gun arm as he began squeezing off shots. The first shot went wild, but the next three went past Elsa and blasted holes in the boat's windshield. Elsa threw an angered glare back at the shooter and saw the other two boats coming up fast behind her. There were three men in one boat and two in the other.

Elsa steered the boat hard to port, and Indy's attacker was thrown off balance. Indy rolled out from under the man and pinned his gun arm before throwing two punches at the man's head. Both punches landed square on his jaw. Indy was still grappling with the man when he glanced up to see that Elsa was steering straight toward a gap that ran between two enormous freighters joined together by thick ropes. A tugboat was pressed up against the outer freighter, pushing the two ships closer together.

"Are you crazy?!" Indy shouted to Elsa. "Don't go between them!"

Elsa could barely hear Indy over the noise of the motor. "Go between them?" she shouted back. "Are you crazy?!" Despite her own cautions, she stayed on course, heading for the increasingly narrow gap between the freighters.

Indy pulled his attacker up and belted him so hard that he sent the man flying overboard. A moment later, the sterns of both freighters suddenly loomed up on either side of the motorboat, and then the boat was racing up the gap. Indy's heart pounded as he scrambled up to the helm. Seizing the wheel from Elsa, he shouted, "I said go *around*!"

"You said go *between* them!" Elsa answered with outrage as she slid aside in the seat and Indy lowered himself behind the wheel.

"I said *don't* go between them!" Indy snapped back. The two freighters were closing in like a massive vise, and there was less than a foot of clearance on either side of Indy's stolen motorboat. Indy kept his eyes forward and focused on the strip of water and sky between the freighters' tapered bows.

While the boat that carried two men steered wide of the freighters, Indy's other pursuers increased speed and followed his path. There was an awful scraping sound as the side of Indy's boat struck the lower hull of one freighter, but as he neared the freighters' bows, the passage widened. Indy and Elsa hadn't realized that they were both holding their breaths until their boat cleared the gap. They gasped simultaneously with relief as they sped away from the freighters.

The three who had followed them weren't so lucky. Indy and Elsa had only just cleared the gap when the freighters crushed the speeding motorboat behind them. The boat exploded, and its momentum sent its fiery hull blasting out between the freighters' bows.

Indy and Elsa were still catching their breaths when they heard the report of gunfire from behind. Glancing back, they saw the other boat was still in pursuit. One man was behind the boat's wheel while the other stood up in the cockpit, firing his weapon in Indy's direction.

The gunner was the same man who had knocked out Marcus Brody and ignited the fire in the catacombs. He stared fiercely after Indy as he continued firing.

Bullets slammed into the stern of Indy's boat, splintering the wood. Hoping to protect Elsa, Indy grabbed the back of her neck and shoved her down against the seat. He hoped that none of the bullets had struck the boat's engine, but then smoke began billowing out from the damaged stern.

The gunfire stopped. Indy didn't know whether the gun had run out of bullets, but he didn't wait around to find out. He angled his boat away and tried to accelerate. Despite his evasive maneuver, his damaged, smoking boat began to lose speed. Even worse, his boat was drifting toward the stern of another freighter, a steamer that had giant, rotating propellers at its stern.

Before Indy could think of what to do next, his pursuers rammed the port aft of his boat. Indy and Elsa glanced back to see that the machine gunner had moved behind the wheel and the other man was seated in the open passenger compartment behind the helm. Returning his gaze to the nearby steamer, Indy realized with mounting panic that their pursuers were trying to send him directly into one of the steamer's propellers.

The machine gunner's boat slid alongside Indy's. When the man in the passenger compartment drew a pistol from his jacket, Indy leaped from his boat and smashed into him, slamming his gun arm into the side of the boat and knocking the pistol from his grip. The other stood up behind the wheel and turned to strike, but Indy turned fast and backhanded him.

As Indy fought the two men, Elsa returned to the controls of the damaged boat and sent it into reverse. Grimacing at the thick black smoke that now poured from the boat's stern, she managed to guide the vessel away from the steamers lethal propeller.

Indy kicked one man overboard, and the man immediately began to swim away from the steamer. The other — the machine gunner who had rammed Indy's boat — threw an arm around Indy's neck. Indy flipped him into the boat's rear compartment, but the man lashed back.

As Indy and his attacker exchanged blows, Elsa looked over from her own boat to see that the men were caught in the drift of the churning water behind the steamer. Elsa gasped. Gripping the shattered windshield, she stood up in the cockpit and screamed, "No!"

Unless Indy did something fast, the steamer's propeller would smash the boat and hack him and his opponent to pieces.

CHAPTER SIX

*I*ndy saw that the boat he had boarded was drifting toward the steamer's enormous propeller, which chopped the water so loudly that he could hardly hear the impact of his fist against his opponent's jaw. The man's red fez fell from his head. Grabbing the lapels of his gray jacket, Indy hauled the man into the cockpit and slammed him down against the seat so he was facing away from the propeller. A moment later, the propeller began hacking at the boat's stern.

As splintered wood flew in all directions, Indy shouted into the man's face, "Why are you trying to kill us?!"

"Because you're looking for the Holy Grail!" the man yelled back.

"My *father* was looking for the Holy Grail!" Indy snarled. "Did you kill him, too?!"

"No," the man answered loudly, not out of fear or anger, but because the propeller was almost deafening.

"Where is he?!" Indy shouted as the propeller continued to savagely reduce the boat's length. Shaking the man violently, Indy said, "Talk or you're dead!"

The man remained silent and made no effort to escape.

"Tell me!" Indy shouted as larger chunks of wood began tearing from the boat. "Tell me!"

Fixing his eyes on Indy's, the man said, "If you don't let go, Dr. Jones, we'll both die."

"Then we'll die," Indy said. The boat continued to feed into the propeller.

"My soul is prepared," the man answered with great composure. "How's yours?"

The propeller was less than eight feet away from the boat's cockpit. Indy said, "This is your last chance."

"No, Dr. Jones," the man said. "It's yours."

If the man knew what had happened to Henry Jones, Indy needed him alive. Indy pulled the man up from the cockpit just as Elsa brought the other boat beside them. The two men leaped into the passenger compartment behind Elsa, and then she accelerated away from the propeller. The rapidly spinning blades quickly consumed the abandoned boat's remains.

Although the surviving motorboat remained visibly damaged, Elsa was able to guide it away from the industrial area and back toward the quieter canals of Venice.

Behind her, Indy faced his captive and said, "All right. Where's my father?"

"If you let me go," the man replied, "I will tell you where he is."

Staring hard into the man's eyes, Indy rasped, "Who are you?"

"My name is Kazim."

"And why are you trying to kill me?"

"The secret of the Grail has been safe for a thousand years," Kazim replied, "and for all that time, the Brotherhood of the Cruciform Sword have been prepared to do anything to keep it safe." Kazim pulled back the collar of his shirt to reveal a tattoo of a cruciform with a tapered end, like the blade of a broadsword. Except for the tapered end, the symbol was nearly identical to the cross that Indy had seen on the Grail tablet and the Grail Knight's shield.

Kazim looked to his right, then returned his gaze to Indy and said, "Let me off at this jetty."

Elsa moved aside as Indy got behind the wheel and steered the boat over to a wooden dock that stretched out from a tall stone building, where an older man watched their approach. Kazim tossed a mooring line to the man and then stepped off the boat and onto the dock. Turning to gaze down at Indy, he said, "Ask yourself, why do you seek the Cup of Christ? Is it for His glory, or for yours?"

"I didn't come for the Cup of Christ," Indy said severely. "I came to find my *father*."

"In that case, God be with you in your quest," Kazim said as he buttoned his jacket. "Your father is being held in the Castle of Brunwald on the Austrian–German border." Then Kazim turned and walked off.

The old man handed the mooring line back into the boat. Indy looked at Elsa with a weary smile. *Well, maybe we're finally getting somewhere.*

After they got rid of the boat, Indy and Elsa went back to the library and found Marcus Brody, who was fine except for a nasty bump on the back of his head. Then they all returned to the apartment that Walter Donovan kept in Venice. Both Indy and Elsa still reeked from their journey through the catacombs and were more than eager to get cleaned up.

After Indy had taken a bath and then a shower and done his best to rid his flesh of the stench of petroleum, he put on a plush green bathrobe and went into the apartment's sitting room to confer with Brody. Brody was sitting on a couch, holding an ice pack against the back of his head. He sat in front of an expensive Chinese coffee table, upon which he had placed Henry Jones's Grail diary. A light breeze came in from the room's open window.

As Indy sat down in a lounge chair beside Brody, he handed over the folded, water-soaked parchment that held the impression of the Grail Knight's shield. Brody still looked a bit dazed as he took the parchment and began to unfold it.

Indy said, "How's the head?"

"It's better, now I've seen this," Brody said as he spread the parchment over the coffee table. Studying the Latin text, he said, "It's the name of a city. 'Alexandretta?' Hmmm . . ."

Indy leaned forward in his chair. While Brody continued to examine the parchment, Indy said, "The Knights of the First Crusade laid siege to the city of Alexandretta for over a year. The entire city was destroyed."

Brody lowered the ice pack, placed it on the table beside the parchment, and looked at Indy.

Indy continued, "The present city of Iskenderun is built on its ruins. Marcus, you remember what the Grail tablet said: 'Across the desert and through the mountain to the Canyon of the Crescent Moon.'" He looked away, thinking. "But where exactly?"

Brody rubbed his hands together, massaging his fingers. He said, "Your father would know."

He probably would, Indy thought, but he answered Brody's comment with a noncommittal, "Mm."

Suddenly, Brody's eyes widened and he exclaimed, "Your father *did* know. Look. He made a map." Brody picked up the Grail diary and began flipping through the pages until he found a map that Henry Jones had drawn. "He must have pieced it together from clues scattered through the whole history of the Grail quest. A map with no names."

Fascinated, Indy leaned in closer.

Brody continued, "Now, he knew there was a city with an oasis due east, here." Brody tapped the position on the map. "He knew the course turned south through the desert to a river, and the river led into the mountains, here. Straight to the canyon." Brody traced the route with his finger. "He knew everything except where to begin, the name of the city."

Indy smiled. "Alexandretta." Clapping his hand on Brody's arm, he said, "Now we know."

"Yes, now we know." Brody was beaming with excitement.

"Marcus, get hold of Sallah," Indy said as he rose from his chair. "Tell him to meet you in Iskenderun."

Indy's friend Sallah was a professional excavator. Brody had met him before. Looking at Indy, Brody said with some concern, "What about you?"

"I'm going after Dad," he said grimly. He took the

Grail diary from Brody, pushed it into one of his robe's deep pockets, and left the sitting room.

Still in his bathrobe, Indy walked to a vestibule that led to his bedroom door. When he opened the door, he found that the room was not at all as he'd left it. Most of the furniture had been overturned, and the bureau drawers had been emptied. Indy felt a sudden burn of anger. *It's just like Dad's house*, he thought. *All over again!*

He heard the muffled sound of music playing on a phonograph from an adjoining room. Elsa's room was next door. *Elsa!*

It had suddenly hit Indy that the person — or people — who had ransacked his room might still be in the building. Leaving his room, he returned to the vestibule and went to another door, the one that led to Elsa's room. He knocked on the door and said in a deliberately calm tone, "Elsa?" As concerned as he was for Elsa's safety, he was also angered by the work and possible presence of the unknown intruder. He didn't wait for a reply, but opened the door and stepped right in.

Elsa's room was also in shambles. Her bureau was a mess, her clothes were strewn across the floor, and framed pictures dangled at odd angles on the wall.

Elsa's room had its own bathroom. The bathroom door was closed. To Indy's ears, the music sounded as if it were coming from the other side of that door. Stepping over the debris, he went to the bathroom door, rapped twice, and said in his still calm-sounding voice, "Elsa?" The music suddenly blared as he opened the door and said again, "Elsa?"

"Oh!" Elsa gasped, startled as she turned away from a mirror and saw Indy. She was wearing a silk bathrobe and had yet to empty the water from her bathtub. The music was coming from a portable phonograph that rested on a windowsill beside the tub.

Indy wagged his finger at Elsa and then retreated from the bathroom. Without a word, she lifted the phonograph's needle off the spinning record and followed Indy into her bedroom. Her jaw dropped open when she saw the awful mess. She seemed to be in shock as she said, "My room . . ."

"Mine, too," Indy said.

"What were they looking for?"

Indy pulled the Grail diary from his pocket. "This."

Elsa's eyes went wide when she saw the book in Indy's hand. Because she had worked with Henry Jones, she recognized the book. "The Grail diary."

"Uh-huh," Indy said as he walked out of Elsa's bedroom, carrying the diary with him.

"You had it?" Elsa asked, following him into the vestibule. Shaking her head as Indy entered his room, she looked hurt as she said, "You didn't trust me."

Turning to face Elsa, who remained standing outside his doorway, Indy said, "I didn't know you. At least I let you tag along."

"Oh, yes," Elsa said as she stepped into his room. "Give them a flower, and they'll follow you anywhere." She slammed the door shut behind her.

Indy's eyes flicked to the closed door, then he faced Elsa and said, "Knock if off. You're not mad."

"No?"

"No." Indy lifted an upturned table from the floor. "You like the way I do things."

"It's lucky I don't do things the same way," Elsa said petulantly. "You'd still be standing at the Venice pier!"

Elsa stomped her foot. Indy flinched. She turned for the door. He grabbed her arm and spun her around to face him.

"Look," Indy said, "what do you think is going on here? Since I met you, I've nearly been incinerated, shot at, and chopped into fish bait. We're caught in the middle of something sinister here. My guess is Dad found out more than he was looking for. And until I'm sure, I'm going to *continue* to do things the way I think they should be done."

Indy reached for the back of Elsa's neck, pulled her face toward his, and kissed her. Elsa pulled her head back and said with a scowl, "How *dare* you kiss me!" Then she reached up with both hands to grab the back of Indy's head, pulling his face toward hers, and kissed him back.

Indy's eyes rolled. He pulled his face away from hers and said with a deadpan expression, "Leave me alone. I don't like fast women."

Indy buried his nose under Elsa's chin. She replied, "And I hate . . . arrogant men."

From outside Indy's open window came the sound of a gondolier's voice, singing as his gondola carried two passengers along the canal outside the building. Hearing the song echo up from the canal, Indy smiled and said, "Ah, Venice."

CHAPTER SEVEN

*T*he day after Brody left Venice for Iskenderun to meet with Sallah, Indy and Elsa left Venice in Elsa's Mercedes-Benz and drove north for Austria. Indy liked the way the car handled and did most of the driving. The following day, storm clouds blew in overhead as they navigated their way up along the high roads of the Austrian mountains to reach Brunwald Castle.

It was raining hard by the time Indy brought the car to a stop in the driveway outside Brunwald, a large, imposing stone structure with a number of soaring turrets that seemed to pierce the dark sky. Indy wore his leather jacket, fedora, safari shirt, khaki pants, and leather boots. He'd added a necktie to his ensemble for the occasion and had brought his gun along. Elsa wore a gray raincoat over a simple dress and a black beret.

Looking at the castle's walls through the car's

rain-streaked windshield, Indy said, "What do you know about this place?"

"I know the Brunwalds are famous art collectors," Elsa replied.

Indy reached into the back seat and picked up his bull-whip. Elsa's eyes went wide at the sight of the whip. She said, "What are you going to do?"

"Don't know," Indy said, coiling the whip. "I'll think of something." He looked at Elsa's face and then lifted his gaze to her beret.

Elsa realized Indy was staring at her beret and reached up to adjust it. Then Indy told her his plan.

A few minutes later, Elsa knocked on the wooden door that functioned as the service entrance. Elsa was wearing Indy's hat on her head and shrugging into his leather jacket when a tall, bald butler in a black suit opened the door and said sharply, "Yes?"

"And not before time!" Indy said from behind Elsa as he pushed her forward and followed her through the door-way. Elsa's coat was draped over Indy's shoulders and her beret rested on his head. Indy had also adopted a Scottish accent, or at least his attempt at one. "Did you intend to leave us standing on the doorstep all day?" he snarled at the butler as he shook the water from the coat on his back. "We're drenched!" Suddenly, Indy sneezed hard in the butler's face. As the butler recoiled, Indy said, "Now look, I've gone and caught a sniffle." He yanked a white handkerchief from the butler's breast pocket and dabbed at his nose.

Clearly irritated, the butler said, "Are you expected?"

"Do not take that tone with me, my good man. Now buttle off and tell Baron Brunwald that Lord Clarce MacDonald and his lovely assistant . . ." — Indy grabbed Elsa's arm and pulled her beside him — ". . . are here to view the tapestries."

"Tapestries?" said the butler incredulously.

Glancing at Elsa, Indy said, "Dear me, the man is dense." Guiding the butler away from the doorway, Indy gestured at the surrounding walls and said, "This is a *castle*, isn't it? There are tapestries?"

"This *is* a castle," the butler answered curtly, "and we have many tapestries. But if you are a Scottish lord, then I am Mickey Mouse!"

Indy looked back over his shoulder at Elsa and said, "How dare he?" Then he spun back at the butler, launching his fist outward to knock the man out cold with a single slug. The butler fell back against the wall, which happened to be adorned with a rather fine old tapestry.

After tucking the unconscious butler into a cupboard, Indy took his hat and jacket back from Elsa and they began exploring the castle. As they moved cautiously down a wide, vaulted hallway, they heard voices from below their position. Peering over a banister, they looked down to see a room full of Nazi soldiers who were working around a large table with a map on it. It looked like a secret Nazi command center.

Lifting his gaze to Elsa, Indy muttered softly, "Nazis. I hate these guys."

While thunder rumbled outside the castle, Indy and Elsa eased away from the banister and continued down the hallway, searching for any sign of Henry Jones. Indy took his gun out of its holster and patted the coiled whip that hung from his belt. Elsa glanced back over her shoulder, and then followed him over to a closed door.

Indy aimed his thumb at the door. "This one. I think he's in here."

"How do you know?"

"Because it's wired," Indy said and raised his thumb to point to the electrical wire that traveled from the top of the door to a small alarm that was mounted above the doorway.

Indy looked to another closed door, a short distance away on the same side of the hallway. The door didn't appear to be wired. Elsa followed Indy as he walked to the door and rapped on it. There was no response. When Indy twisted the doorknob, he found it was unlocked.

Holding his gun out in front of him, Indy entered a dark, empty room. Light was coming in through a rain-spattered window. Followed by Elsa, Indy holstered his gun as he walked straight to the window and opened it, letting rain into the room. He climbed up onto the wet windowsill, and then he stepped onto a ledge outside the window. He leaned out to peer out at the castle walls and look for a route to the neighboring room. When he found something that looked good, he reached for his bullwhip.

"Indy?" Elsa said, watching with mounting concern as he uncoiled the whip. "Indy!"

"Don't worry . . . this is kid's play," Indy said. "I'll be right back."

Indy threw his bullwhip out so that its end wrapped around some wires protruding from the castle wall above the window to the neighboring room. He gave the whip a forceful tug to make certain it would hold his weight, and then leaped away from his position. He swung through the air and landed on a stone gargoyle that jutted out from a nearby turret.

As he stood atop the gargoyle, Indy looked back to see Elsa leaning out of the window that he'd just left. He shifted his body, angling to swing toward a shuttered window to the right of Elsa. He knew that the room with the alarmed door was on the other side of the shutters.

Gripping his whip tightly, he leaped out again, swinging away from the gargoyle and straight for the shuttered window with his feet extended.

A clap of thunder drowned out the loud crash of Indy's body hurtling through the shutters and window. Wood splintered and glass shattered as he landed inside the room. Rain and cold air whipped through the smashed window behind him. He gasped as he rose from the debris on the floor.

No sooner was Indy on his feet than a large vase came crashing down on top of his head. Although his hat absorbed some of the impact, his skull still took the brunt of it. He fell to his knees with a stunned, dazed expression.

A bespectacled man with a gray beard and mustache stepped out from the shadows behind Indy. The man wore a tweed suit and hat. His brow furrowed as he looked down at Indy. "Junior?"

Jumping to his feet to face his attacker, Indy responded automatically to the sound of his father's voice. "Yes, sir." Indeed, the man who'd struck Indy was Dr. Henry Jones.

Facing his son, Henry smiled. "It *is* you, Junior!"

Indy's shoulders sagged. "Don't call me that, *please*."

The room in which Henry was being held captive was relatively small. Except for some German words engraved in the molding above the wooden doorway, there were few remarkable architectural details and even fewer comforts. The furniture included a wooden desk with a lamp on it, a chair, and a bench built into the wall. As rain continued to pour in through the ruined window, Henry said, "Well, what are you doing here?"

"I came to get you. What do you thi —?"

From outside the window came the sound of voices approaching. Indy threw his arm across Henry's chest, and they both pressed themselves against the wall. As Indy cautiously stepped toward the window to look at the grounds below, Henry lifted his right hand and realized he was still gripping the handle of the vase — or rather the remains of the vase — that he'd brought down on Indy's head. Henry's eyes widened with dismay.

While Indy remained by the window, Henry carried the ruined vase over to the desk and held it under the lamp to examine its broken edges more closely. "Late fourteenth century, Ming Dynasty," he observed with a frown. "Oh, it breaks the heart."

"And the head," Indy said, leaving the window. Rubbing the back of his skull, he added, "You hit me, Dad."

Lifting his gaze from the vase, Henry said, "I'll never forgive myself."

What? Indy could hardly believe his ears. "Don't worry," he said with a smile. "I'm fine."

"Thank God," Henry said and gently reached out to take his son's arm and pull him closer to the desk. Then Henry pointed to the exposed interior of the broken vase and said with a grin, "It's a fake."

Indy had thought that his father had been expressing remorse for clobbering him, but he suddenly realized that his father wasn't concerned about him at all. Indy's smile vanished as he redirected his gaze to the vase.

"See," Henry continued, "you can tell by the cross section."

Indy nodded.

Obviously pleased with himself for having determined that he hadn't destroyed an actual Ming vase, Henry — without any concern about alerting his captors — tossed the damaged vase at the wall.

"No!" Indy shouted, but too late. The vase crashed against the wall, and its pieces clattered against the floor.

"Dad, get your stuff," Indy said. "We've got to get out of here."

Indy knew his father couldn't make it out through the window and that they wouldn't get far if they tried opening the wired door either. While Indy looked for another way out, Henry turned to pick up his umbrella and a leather bag that contained a few other belongings. As Henry sat down in a chair near the window, he said, "Well, I'm sorry about your head, though, but I thought you were one of them."

"Dad, *they* come in through the *doors*."

Henry glanced at the door and laughed, "Heh! Good point. But better safe than sorry."

Indy didn't reply as he examined the room's other doors. All were locked.

"Humph," Henry said, "so I was wrong this time. But, by God, I wasn't wrong when I mailed you my diary." He slid his umbrella through the straps of his bag, which he'd placed on his lap. "You obviously got it."

Walking back to stand beside the desk, Indy looked at his seated father across the room. "I got it, and I used it," Indy said. "We found the entrance to the catacombs."

In a hushed, excited voice, Henry said, "Through the library?"

Indy smiled and nodded. "Right."

Keeping his eyes on Indy, Henry stood up. "I knew it," he said. "And the tomb of Sir Richard?"

Indy nodded again. "Found it."

Carrying his bag and umbrella before him, Henry stepped quietly across the room to stand before his son. "He was actually there? You saw him?"

"Well, what was left of him," Indy said.

Henry's eyes were riveted on Indy's. "And his shield . . ." Henry said, "the inscription on Sir Richard's shield?"

Indy grinned. "Alexandretta."

"Alexandretta!" Henry exclaimed as he dropped his bag on top of the desk. He spun away and walked in a circle as he pulled off his hat. "Of course!" He stopped to face Indy and said, "On the pilgrim trail from the Eastern Empire. Oh . . ." Smiling broadly, Henry sat back down on a wooden bench against the wall, looked up to his son and said, "Junior, you did it."

"No, Dad," Indy said. "You did. Forty years."

Shaking his head, Henry sighed, "Oh, if only I could have been with you."

"There were rats, Dad," Indy said, placing his hand on his father's arm to urge him up from the bench.

"Rats?" Henry said meekly.

"Yeah, big ones," Indy said as he guided his father back to the desk. "What do the Nazis want with you, Dad?"

Placing his hat back on his head, Henry said, "They wanted my diary."

"Yeah?"

Checking his bag, Henry said, "I knew I had to get that book as far away from me as I possibly could."

Indy hadn't imagined or realized that his father *didn't* want the Grail diary returned to him. Turning his head slowly to look away from his father, Indy said, "Yeah," while he thought, *Uh-oh*. But before he could think of whether he should explain to his father that he was carrying the Grail diary in the pocket of his leather jacket at that very moment, there was a sudden *wham* from the doorway as the door was kicked open, followed by a *thud* as it slammed into the wall.

Indy and Henry looked to the open doorway to see a Nazi S.S. officer holding a machine gun. The officer stepped into the room, followed by two Nazi soldiers who also held machine guns.

Indy raised his hands. Henry glanced at Indy and followed his example.

The S.S. officer glared at them. "Dr. Jones."

"Yes?" Indy and Henry answered simultaneously.

The S.S. officer aimed his machine gun at Indy and said, "I will take the book now."

Indy and his father looked at each other, then both replied, "What book?"

Keeping his eyes fixed on Indy, the officer said, "You have the diary in your pocket."

Henry laughed at the officer. "You dolt!" he said. "Do you think my son would be that *stupid* that he would bring my diary all the way back here?" Henry grinned as he turned his head to face Indy, but his grin vanished when he saw Indy's sheepish expression. Henry said, "You didn't, did you? You didn't *bring* it, did you?"

Indy felt his throat go dry. "Well, uh . . ."

"You *did*," Henry said.

Gesturing at the Nazi soldiers, Indy said, "Look, can we discuss this later?"

Glowering, Henry said, "I should have mailed it to the Marx Brothers."

"Will you take it easy?" Indy said, lowering his voice.

"Take it easy?!" Henry roared in return. "Why do you think I sent it home in the first place? So it wouldn't fall into their hands!" He gestured at the Nazi soldiers, who kept their guns trained on him and Indy.

Staring hard at his father, Indy shouted back, "I came here to save you!"

"Oh, yeah?" Henry said, "And who's gonna come to save you, Junior?!"

Indy's eyes blazed and nostrils flared. "I *told* you . . ." Indy snarled with rage, and then interrupted himself by stepping forward to grab the S.S. officer's machine gun. Shoving the officer backwards, Indy slid his finger over the gun's trigger and opened fire on the Nazis. Henry Jones cringed at the noise and gaped in astonishment as the officer and two soldiers went down. Only after the Nazis lay dead on the floor did Indy turn to face his father and complete his sentence: ". . . *don't* call me Junior!"

Indy grabbed his father's arm and tugged him toward the doorway. Still gaping, Henry glanced down at the fallen soldiers. "Look what you did!" He was genuinely aghast. "I can't believe what you did. . . ."

Clutching the machine gun, Indy led his father down the corridor to the next door, which led to room where he had left Elsa. "Elsa?" Indy said as he opened the door and stepped in. "Elsa?" And then he saw her.

Elsa's eyes were wide with fear. A black-uniformed, blue-eyed Nazi colonel named Vogel stood behind Elsa, pinning her arms behind her back with one hand while the other pressed the muzzle of a Luger pistol against her head.

"That's far enough," Vogel said as Henry followed Indy into the room. "Put down the gun, Dr. Jones. Put down the gun, or the fräulein dies."

As Vogel held Elsa in front of him like a shield, Henry glanced at Indy and said, "But she's one of *them*."

Trembling in Vogel's grip, Elsa cried, "Indy, please!"

Henry raised his voice. "She's a Nazi!"

"What?!" Indy snapped, keeping his gaze on Elsa.

"Trust me," Henry said.

Elsa screamed, "Indy, no!"

"I will kill her!" Vogel said as he pressed his pistol's muzzle hard against Elsa's lower jaw.

"Yeah?" Henry said casually. "Go ahead."

"No!" Indy shouted at the colonel. "Don't shoot!"

"Don't worry," Henry said. "He won't."

"Indy, please!" Elsa cried desperately. "Do what he says!"

Henry added, "And don't listen to *her*."

"Enough!" Vogel shouted. "She dies!"

Elsa screamed again.

"Wait!" Indy shouted. Then he lowered his voice and said again, "Wait . . ." There was a table to his right. He placed the machine gun on the table and shoved it down toward the colonel.

Vogel re-aimed his pistol at Indy and then pushed Elsa away from him. Elsa was propelled directly into Indy's arms. He held her tightly against him, and then she drew back to look up into his eyes. She whimpered, "I'm sorry."

"No," Indy said, "don't be." He hadn't believed his father's assertion that Elsa was a Nazi, so he could hardly blame her for their situation. He gave her what he hoped was a comforting smile.

And then Elsa looked down to one of Indy's jacket pockets. Indy lowered his head to follow her gaze, then watched with astonishment as she dipped her hand into his pocket and removed the Grail diary.

Stunned speechless, Indy glared at Elsa. Her lips curved into a smile as she backed away from him, taking the diary with her. She said, "But . . . you should have listened to your father." She was still smiling as she returned to Vogel's side. Vogel kept his pistol trained on Indy.

Indy looked away from Elsa. He was still speechless.

He kept his gaze averted from his father, too.

CHAPTER EIGHT

Colonel Vogel, Elsa, and several armed Nazi soldiers escorted Indy and Henry to a large baronial room within the castle. A long wooden table with benches on either side stretched the length of the room, which was decorated with ancient tapestries, displays of swords, and suits of armor. Old rugs with ornate designs rested on the floor. A giant fireplace, nearly large enough for a man to stand upright within it, dominated one wall, and the fire cast flickering shadows across the walls and ceiling.

The soldiers had taken away Indy's weapons and his father's bag and umbrella, and had tied the two men's hands behind their backs. Inside the baronial room, the soldiers maneuvered their bound captives to stand near one end of the long table.

Carrying the diary, Elsa brazenly brushed past Indy and Henry, and walked toward the fireplace. Indy glanced at his father and muttered, "She ransacked her own room, and I fell for it."

Elsa walked over to a tall, wooden wingback chair that was positioned to face the fireplace. Because of the angle, Indy and Henry could not see who was sitting in the chair, but as Elsa stepped beside the chair and held the diary out, they did see a hand reach up to take the diary.

Looking to his father, Indy said, "How did you know she was a Nazi?"

"Hmm?"

Leaning closer to Henry, Indy repeated, "How did you know she was a Nazi?"

As Indy returned his gaze to Elsa and the mysterious person in the wingback chair, Henry replied, "She talks in her sleep."

Indy gave a slight nod to acknowledge that he'd heard his father, but it took a few seconds longer for that information to sink in. When it did, Indy looked at his father with surprise. Henry smiled sheepishly, looked at the floor for a moment, then returned his gaze to his son and said, "*I* didn't trust her. Why did *you*?"

"Because he *didn't* take my advice," came a man's voice from the wingback chair. And then the man, who wore an expensive gray three-piece suit, rose from the chair. Holding the diary, he turned and walked slowly toward Indy. The man was Walter Donovan.

"Donovan," Indy said with a scowl. Henry Jones had also had dealings with Donovan and recognized him, too.

Gazing at Indy, Donovan said, "Didn't I warn you not to trust *anybody*, Dr. Jones?"

As Donovan began thumbing through the pages of the diary, Henry said, "I misjudged you, Walter. I knew you'd sell your mother for an Etruscan vase, but I didn't know you would sell your country and your soul . . . to the slime of humanity." Henry fixed his gaze on Elsa and the smirking Colonel Vogel.

"Dr. Schneider!" Donovan said. "There are pages torn out of this."

While Elsa took the book from Donovan and examined it, Indy grinned slightly and exchanged a glance with his father. Henry had no idea that any pages had been removed from his diary and looked baffled.

Elsa looked at Indy. Holding the book up as she walked toward him, she said, "This book contained a map, a map with no names, precise directions from the unknown city to the secret Canyon of the Crescent Moon."

"So it did," Indy said flatly.

From behind Elsa, Donovan said peevishly, "*Where* are these missing pages, this map? We must have these pages back."

Elsa shook her head. Glancing back at Donovan, she said, "You're wasting your breath." Returning her gaze to

Indy, she continued, "He won't tell us, and he doesn't have to. It's perfectly obvious where the pages are. He's given them to Marcus Brody."

"Marcus?" Henry gasped. He and Brody were both members of the University Club and had known each other for years. Glaring at Indy, he said, "You didn't drag poor Marcus along, did you? He's not up to the challenge."

"He sticks out like a sore thumb," Donovan said. "We'll find him."

"Fat chance," Indy said with bravado. "He's got a two-day head start on you, which is more than he needs. Brody's got friends in every town and village from here to the Sudan. He speaks a dozen languages, knows every local custom. He'll blend in, disappear. You'll never see him again. With any luck, he's got the Grail already."

Hearing this, Henry Jones looked amazed and impressed. Either there was much more to Marcus Brody than Henry realized, or his son was talking about a completely different person.

"Does anyone here speak English?" Marcus Brody asked feebly as he waded through the crowd on a Turkish train platform. "Or even ancient Greek?"

He had just disembarked the train in the city of Iskenderun, on the Mediterranean coast of Turkey, and was surrounded by merchants and traders as well as passengers. Wearing a straw hat and pale gray suit and carrying a set of battered luggage, Brody did indeed stick out like a sore thumb.

A man held a water-filled stein out to Brody, who said, "Uh, water? No, thank you, sir." As more goods were shoved in his face by various merchants, he politely but loudly refused everything. "Goodness me. Thank you so much. No, I don't like that. No, I really don't want . . . No, no, thank you very much." When a woman thrust a clucking chicken before him, he replied, "No, thank you, madam. I'm a vegetarian." The chicken fluttered, and Brody's suit and face were suddenly adorned with small feathers.

Dazed by the heat, overwhelmed by everything and everyone around him, Brody came to a stop and muttered, "Does anyone understand a word I'm saying here?"

"Mr. Brody!" said a voice from behind.

Brody turned to face Sallah, who was wearing a red fez and a rumpled white linen suit. Sallah beamed as he embraced Brody.

"Oh, Sallah," Brody sighed as Sallah brushed the feathers from his face and jacket. "What a relief."

"Marcus Brody, sir!" Sallah said brightly as he took Brody's luggage. Then, cocking his head slightly, he added, "But where is Indy?"

"Oh, he's in Austria," Brody replied. "A slight detour."

"You are on your own?"

"Yes, but don't panic," Brody said. "Everything's under control." As they walked out of the busy train station, he said, "Have you . . . have you arranged our supplies?"

"Oh, yes, of course," Sallah answered. "But where are we *going*?"

"Oh, this map will show you," Brody said as he reached for the folded map in his jacket's breast pocket. "It was drawn by, uh . . ."

Brody saw two fair-skinned men approaching them. Both men wore black suits and hats. The man on the right wore dark wire-frame glasses and black leather gloves, and had a matching leather coat draped over his left arm. The second man was in his shirtsleeves and had his jacket slung over his shoulder. Brody quickly tucked the map back into his pocket as the bespectacled man stopped before him.

"Mr. Brody," the man said, clicking his heels together and then bowing quickly. "Welcome to Iskenderun. The director of the Museum of Antiquities has sent a car for you."

"Oh, well..." Brody said, removing his hat in an appreciative gesture. "Your servant, sir."

"And I am his," Sallah interjected as he leaned close to Brody.

Baring his teeth in a strained smile, the bespectacled man bowed to Sallah and then said, "Follow me, please."

The two men in black suits turned away from the station and Brody and Sallah began following them. Brody had been so honored to receive an official greeting that he failed to think anything of the bespectacled man's German accent. Smiling smugly, Brody said, "My reputation precedes me."

"There is no museum in Iskenderun," Sallah said under his breath.

But the second man, the one in his shirtsleeves, heard. Turning fast, the second man held out his hand to Sallah and said in an official tone, "Papers, please."

"Papers?" Sallah said. Then he smiled at the two men and said, "Of course." But as he bent down to place Brody's luggage on the ground, he tilted his head slightly to face Brody and said, "Run."

But Brody, still oblivious to the fact that he might be in any danger, said absently, "Yes."

"Papers," Sallah said as he stood up and patted his pockets. "Got it here." He pulled out a folded newspaper and held it up for the men to see. "Just finished reading it myself," he said, laughing. Tossing another glance at Brody, he repeated, "Run."

"Yes," Brody said, even though he still didn't understand what Sallah meant by the word.

Sallah held up the newspaper so that the man in shirtsleeves could see the masthead. Still smiling, Sallah said, "'Egyptian Mail,' morning edition." Gritting his teeth, he barely moved his lips as he glanced at Brody again and desperately muttered, "Run."

Leaning closer to Sallah, Brody said, "Did you say, uh . . ."

"Run!" Sallah shouted as he threw a punch through the raised newspaper to hit the second man. As the man stumbled back and fell over a nearby vendor's table, Sallah grabbed the bespectacled man and hurled him into another table.

A crowd gathered around the fight immediately. Even then, Brody didn't run, but stood at the edge of the crowd, watching Sallah with amazement. Brody probably would have remained there had Sallah not run toward him, grabbed his arm, and pulled him aside.

With Brody in tow, Sallah pushed his way past the fight's spectators and ran a short distance up the crowded street. When Sallah sighted a ramp that led up to a building's dark, curtained doorway, he shouted, "Okay, okay, quick, quick, quick!" He guided Brody onto the ramp and added, "Find the back door! Find the back door!"

As Brody stepped up the ramp, past the curtains, and into the doorway, Sallah — expecting that he and Brody had been followed by the men in dark suits — turned around and raised his fists, ready for another fight. But a moment later, he heard the sound of an engine start and a door slam behind him.

Sallah turned around to face the building just in time to see that it wasn't a building at all, but merely a wide, arched doorway. Two men had raised the ramp, which was actually the rear hatch of a troop truck. On the back of the hatch was a painted swastika.

Sallah bolted after the truck, but it tore off, leaving him in a cloud of dust, and standing in an empty archway. Feeling utterly defeated, Sallah slumped against the archway's inner wall and watched the truck vanish in the distance.

He had lost Marcus Brody to the Nazis.

CHAPTER NINE

*B*ack at Brunwald Castle, Indy and Henry's circumstances had hardly improved. They were still in the baronial chamber with the large fireplace, where two soldiers had tied them back-to-back in a pair of chairs. Henry's hands remained tied behind his back, but Indy's wrists had been retied in front of him to prevent the two men from attempting to untie each other's bonds. Even their legs were bound, leaving only their heads with some range of motion. The fire in the fireplace had gone out, leaving a chill in the room.

Elsa Schneider and Walter Donovan stood nearby. They had watched the two soldiers tie up the American captives and now waited for Colonel Vogel to return from the radio room. As the soldiers stepped away from Indy and Henry, Henry muttered out of the side of his mouth, "Intolerable."

The soldiers were walking out of the room just as Vogel returned. Striding toward Elsa, he said, "Dr. Schneider. Message from Berlin. You must return immediately. A rally at the Institute of Aryan Culture."

Neither impressed nor intrigued, Elsa said, "So?"

"Your presence on the platform is requested . . . at the highest level."

Addressing Vogel by his Army rank, Elsa said, "Thank you, Herr Oberst." Then she turned to Donovan and said, "I will meet you at Iskenderun."

Donovan handed the Grail diary to Elsa. "Take this diary to the Reich Museum in Berlin. It will show them our progress, ahead of schedule. Without a map, I'm afraid it's no better than a souvenir."

Vogel eyed Indy and Henry, bound and helpless just a short distance away, then glanced at Donovan and Elsa and said, "Let me kill them now."

"No," Elsa said. "If we fail to recover the pages from Brody, we'll need them alive."

Donovan shrugged. "Always do what the doctor orders." Then Donovan walked out of the room with Vogel at his heels, leaving Elsa alone with Indy and Henry.

From his chair, Indy stared hard at Elsa. He was angry at himself, but was even angrier with *her*. She had misled him from the beginning and betrayed him with ease.

She was obviously intelligent, brave, and beautiful, but there was no getting around the fact that she was far more dangerous than any snake Indy had ever encountered.

And Indy hated snakes.

Elsa looked at Indy, bound to his chair, and felt the burn in his gaze. "Don't look at me like that," she said. "We both wanted the Grail. I would have done anything to get it." Holding the Grail diary out as if it were a trophy she had earned fairly, she smiled as she added, "You would have done the same."

"I'm sorry you think so."

Stung by Indy's words, Elsa's smile vanished and she drew back. But then she smiled again and bent forward to run her hand down the side of Indy's face. As Indy strained against his ropes, trying to pull away from her, she whispered into his ear, "I can't forget . . . how wonderful you are."

Because Henry and Indy remained seated back-to-back, and because their heads were only a short distance apart, Henry heard Elsa's whispered words. Thinking she was speaking to him, Henry replied, "Thank you."

Surprised by his father's response, Indy began to twist his head to look at Henry, but Elsa grabbed Indy's chin and kissed him. Henry sensed the sudden quiet behind him and turned his head slightly to see Elsa kissing his son. With some disappointment, Henry winced as he turned his head back to face forward.

Just then, Vogel returned to the room to remind Elsa of her appointment in Berlin. Vogel saw Elsa kissing Indy and said curtly, "Oh, Dr. Schneider. Your car is waiting."

Elsa dragged out the kiss a moment longer, and then pulled away from Indy's face. Standing before him with a satisfied smile, she said, "That's how Austrians say good-bye." Then she walked off, taking the Grail diary with her.

As Elsa left the room, Vogel stepped in front of Indy and looked down at the bound man. With an evil leer, Vogel said, "And this is how we say good-bye in Germany, Dr. Jones."

Vogel punched Indy in the jaw. It was a hard and vicious jab that snapped Indy's head back and to the side. His head struck Henry's, who gasped, "Oh!"

Vogel followed Elsa out of the room. Indy shook his head clear. "Ooooh . . ." he groaned. "I liked the Austrian way better."

"So did I," Henry admitted.

"Let's try and get these ropes loose," Indy said as he began wiggling his fingers against his bonds. "We've got to get to Marcus before the Nazis do!"

Confused, Henry said, "You said he had two days' start. That he would blend in. Disappear!"

"Are you kidding?" Indy said. "I made that up. You know Marcus. He got lost once in his own museum."

"Oh . . ." Henry sighed as he lowered his head with dismay.

Squirming in his seat, Indy said, "Can you try and reach into my left jacket pocket?" Then both men were squirming, struggling against the ropes, until Henry was able to wiggle his hand toward Indy's coat pocket.

Henry said, "What am I looking for?

"My lucky charm."

Removing a small, metallic object from Indy's pocket, Henry said, "Feels like a cigarette lighter."

In fact, it was Elsa's lighter, the one with the four-leaf clover design. Indy had hung onto it since Elsa had let him use it in the catacombs in Venice. Indy said, "Try and burn through the ropes."

"Very good," Henry said. Because of the way that the ropes pinned his upper arms to his torso, he couldn't actually see the lighter in his hand, but his fingers managed to open the lighter and ignite the flame. Unfortunately, as he tried to angle the flame towards the ropes, the flame met his flesh. "Oh!" he yelped as his fingers reflexively dropped the lighter, which fell on the rug, just in front of his right shoe.

It was bad enough that Henry had dropped the lighter on the old rug, but even worse, it continued to burn. While Indy kept trying to loosen the ropes, Henry tried to kick the lighter away from his foot, which wasn't exactly easy — his legs were bound, too. Unable to reach the lighter with the tip of his shoe, he tilted his chin down and began blowing at the flames. Although Henry Jones was a highly intelligent man, he did not stop to think that this action might actually fan the flames and cause them to spread across the old rug, which was exactly what happened.

Henry watched with dread as the flames spread from the rug to the nearby wooden table and bench. Behind him, Indy remained oblivious to the blaze. As the table and bench ignited, Henry said over his shoulder, "I ought to tell you something."

"Don't get sentimental now, Dad," Indy said, still unaware that half the room was on fire. "Save it 'til we get out of here."

"The floor's on fire," Henry said. "See?"

"What?" Indy said as he craned his neck to confirm that the floor in front of Henry was blazing.

"*And* the chair," Henry added.

"Move!" Indy shouted as he began jerking his body to his right. "Move it out of here! Go!" Henry echoed Indy's movement, rocking the legs of their chairs to inch away from the flames and off the burning carpet.

"It's scorching the table," Henry observed.

"Move!" Indy commanded.

"Okay!" Henry said, eager to comply.

Outside the castle, a moment after Elsa was driven away in a black sedan, Vogel opened the rear door of another waiting car and Donovan stepped past him and climbed in. A moment after Vogel closed the door, a Nazi lieutenant walked up beside the door. "*Etwas wichtig, mein Herr*," the lieutenant said as he handed a written message through the door's open window to Donovan.

Still standing outside the car, Vogel leaned down beside the open window as Donovan read the message. "Well, we have Marcus Brody," Donovan said. "But more important, we have the map."

As the lieutenant returned inside the castle, a radio operator stepped up to Donovan's car with yet another message. "*Aus Berlin, mein Herr.*"

Donovan took the message and read aloud, "'By the personal command of the Führer. Secrecy essential to success. Eliminate the American conspirators.'" Lowering the message, Donovan said to Vogel, "Germany has declared war on the Jones boys." Then Donovan caught his driver's eye in the car's rear view mirror and said, "*Los fahren.*"

As Donovan's car pulled away from the castle, Vogel grinned. He had been looking forward to eliminating the Americans, especially the younger one, and now he could do it on the Führer's orders.

Vogel turned and walked straight back into the castle.

The baronial room was rapidly becoming a wall-to-wall inferno. The hanging tapestries and most of the wooden furniture were blazing away, launching cinders in all directions. Still tied back-to-back, Indy and Henry maneuvered their chairs away from the flames. Indy looked to his right and saw that one of the few areas *not* on fire was inside the large fireplace.

"Dad!" Indy shouted.

"What?" Henry replied and turned his head to his left.

But Indy, thinking his father hadn't heard him over the roaring fire, turned his own head in the opposite direction and shouted again, "Dad!"

Turning the other way, Henry shouted louder, "What?"

"Dad!" shouted Indy, turning again.

"What?"

When he and his father were finally looking in the same direction, Indy yelled, "Head for the fireplace!"

"Oh," Henry said.

Banging, rocking, and hopping their chairs, they

worked their way into the fireplace. As Indy looked down at his bound wrists and wiggled his fingers, he said, "I think I can get these ropes off." But as he struggled to free his hands, his foot kicked out and accidentally hit the nearest andiron. Indy didn't know it, but this particular andiron did more than hold logs within the fireplace. As he hit the andiron again, there was a clicking sound, and then the fireplace floor began to rotate like a carousel.

Indy said, "Whoops!"

Moving counter-clockwise, the rotating floor carried Indy and Henry around in a tight circle and revealed that the baronial chamber adjoined a Nazi radio room that was without windows. It was a different room from the one Indy had seen earlier, shortly after he had entered the castle with Elsa, but like that room, there was a table with a map on it. As the fireplace floor rotated, Indy quickly counted five people in the room, including a radioman wearing headphones who sat at an elaborate panel of dials, switches, and meters, and a woman who monitored the map on a table. Speaking in German, the woman appeared to be plotting coordinates for other soldiers. All of the Nazis had their backs turned to the fireplace and failed to notice Indy or Henry, who remained silent as the carousel carried them a full 360 degrees. When the carousel came to a stop, Indy and Henry had been returned to the blazing chamber.

"Our situation has not improved," Henry said grimly.

"Listen, Dad," Indy said, "I'm almost free." But as Indy continued to loosen the ropes at his wrists, his leg accidentally struck the andiron again, but just a single time. As the fireplace floor began to rotate, Indy suddenly realized that the andiron was the mechanism that activated the carousel. But because he had only hit the andiron once this time, the carousel did not turn completely on its axis, but instead carried Henry and Indy around to face the radio room before it came to an abrupt stop.

Indy and Henry sat very still, but their intrusion did not go unnoticed by the woman who stood beside the map on the table. While the men in the room continued to focus on their controls, the woman, who'd felt a wave of heat travel from the wall behind her, turned her head slowly to face the two Americans. She gazed at them with a surprised, puzzled expression.

Knowing they were completely vulnerable, Indy and Henry smiled sheepishly at the woman. A slightly nervous smile crept across her face, and then she screamed at the top of her lungs, "Alarm!"

The four radiomen jumped as they turned to see Henry and Indy. Suddenly, an alarm began ringing loudly. The woman yelled, "*Schnell!*"

As two of the radiomen reached for their holstered pistols, Indy deliberately threw the side of his leg against the andiron, and the fireplace floor began to rotate again. The radiomen fired several rounds at Indy and Henry, but they missed and the bullets pinged off against the closing door.

When the carousel came to a stop, Indy and Henry were delivered back to the baronial chamber. Every piece of furniture was ablaze, and the flames that reached up to the ceiling had transformed the room into a massive broiler. Henry grumbled loudly, "This is intolerable!"

Just then, Indy pulled his wrists free from the ropes and declared, "I'm out, Dad!"

"Well done, boy!" Henry said.

Meanwhile, in the radio room, all four radiomen had their guns drawn. Their female counterpart motioned them to stand near the secret door before she drew her own pistol. One of the men activated the mechanism to open the secret door, and it swiveled open halfway, so that the dividing wall stopped at a perpendicular angle within the fireplace.

Three radiomen and the woman moved cautiously through the open passage and into the burning room. On the floor in front of the fireplace, they found two overturned chairs and a few small piles of rope. They squinted at the flames, but couldn't see any sign of the escaped Americans.

Indy and Henry had not even attempted to flee through the inferno, but had concealed themselves within the chimney above the fireplace. They both dropped down at the same time, landing behind the radiomen, who continued to face the opposite direction, searching the burning room. Indy and Henry were about to jump back into the radio room when Indy was tackled by the lone radioman who had not entered the burning chamber.

The man locked his arm around Indy's neck, and Indy reached down to slam the andiron mechanism forward. As the rotating floor turned, leaving a frightened-looking Henry temporarily behind, Indy knocked out his attacker with a single punch and left the man slumped against the dividing wall. A moment later, the carousel carried Henry around to Indy's side, and the knocked-out radioman was delivered to his allies.

In the radio room with his father, Indy heard a clicking sound and realized the radiomen were trying to activate the secret door again. The radiomen had already tried to shoot him and Henry, and he wasn't about to give them another chance. Thinking quickly, he reached for the nearest object he could grab, a small bust of Adolf Hitler that rested on top of a shelf. Indy shoved the bust forward to jam the rotating wall in place, sealing the Nazis inside the burning chamber.

On a table in the radio room, Indy found his whip, the sack that contained his gun, and his father's bag and umbrella. Indy grabbed his things and shoved the other stuff at his father. "Come on, Dad!"

The radio room had only one exit, and they took it. They ran through an L-shaped corridor that led them straight into an empty room with a vaulted ceiling. Daylight seeped in through a few small, barred windows, but the windows were so covered with grime that Indy couldn't see outside. His eyes swept the room and found it was without any doors.

"Dead end," Indy said. He knew it was only a matter of time before more soldiers came in response to the alarm from the radio room. Searching frantically for an exit, he said, "There's got to be a . . . a secret door or a . . . passage-way or something."

In the middle of the room, Henry walked around in a circle as he followed Indy's movement. While Indy ran his hands over the walls and tried to find anything resem-bling a concealed passage, Henry noticed a chair that rested near a circular arrangement of inlaid stones in the floor. Indy had just set foot on the stones when Henry eased himself down onto the chair and said, "I find that if I just sit down and think . . ."

As Henry sat, the chair tilted back with a creak and a click. Suddenly, the stones beneath Indy's feet slid downwards and transformed into a spiral staircase. Indy tried to right himself but tumbled down the stone steps and hollered, "Dad!"

Still seated in the chair, Henry saw his son fall down the staircase that had appeared. Staring in amazement at the staircase, Henry completed his thought with some satisfaction: ". . . the solution presents itself." He got up from the chair and climbed down the steps after his son.

Indy had only suffered a few bruises from the staircase, which delivered him and his father to a cavern beneath the mountain on which the castle was built. The cavern opened to the edge of a river, where the Nazis had set up a boat dock for receiving supplies.

The previous day's storm had passed, and the sky was almost as blue as the three supply boats moored beside the dock. Remembering his recent chase through the canals of Venice, Indy muttered, "Great. More boats."

He quickly inspected several large crates that rested on the dock and then jumped into one of the boats. As Indy started the boat's outboard engine, Henry walked to the edge of the dock. "You say this has been just another typical day for you, huh?" He tossed his bag to Indy.

"Oof!" Indy gasped as he caught the heavy bag. Throwing it back at his father, he answered, "No! But better than most." Indy left the boat's engine running as he jumped back onto the dock. After bending down to release the boat's mooring line, he turned and moved quickly down the dock. "Come on, Dad," he urged. "Come on!"

"What about the boat?" Henry said as the empty boat began moving away from the dock. "We're not going on the boat?" Baffled, he followed his son.

Colonel Vogel had failed to reach the castle's baronial room or the concealed radio room before Henry Jones and his arrogant son had escaped, but Vogel knew the castle's layout well enough to know that they only had one way out: the spiral staircase, if they could find it. As he led a squad of soldiers out of the radio room and into the adjoining room with the vaulted ceiling, he nearly seethed when he saw the hidden staircase had been accessed.

Vogel and his men descended the staircase and ran out onto the riverside loading dock. Seeing that one of the motorboats had left the dock and was traveling up the river, he turned to the six soldiers behind him and barked, "*Sie alle ins boat! Schnell!*"

Following Vogel's command, the six soldiers scrambled into one of the remaining boats. None of them even glanced at any of the large crates on the dock. Just as Vogel leaped into the back of the boat, the side of one of the larger crates fell open to reveal its contents: a motorbike with a sidecar, as well as the two escapees.

Indy was already seated on the motorbike and his father was in the sidecar that was mounted on the bike's right side. Indy gunned the engine and they raced across the dock. Vogel turned and saw them, and then howled with rage. As the motorbike roared past the dock and through a small tunnel, two Nazi soldiers jumped out in front of the tunnel. Indy rammed them, sending them falling into the river, and then accelerated onto a dirt road.

Indy glanced back and saw that Vogel had jumped off the boat and was shouting orders from the dock. Indy exclaimed, "Ha!" as he and his father raced away from the castle. He grinned as he looked at his father beside him, but when he saw Henry Jones's worried expression, he returned his gaze to the tree-lined road ahead.

A moment after Indy rounded a bend in the road, he and his father heard loud engines approaching from behind. Glancing back over their shoulders, they saw four Nazi soldiers on motorcycles in hot pursuit. The soldiers had machine guns slung over their shoulders.

Henry gasped as Indy twisted the throttle, throwing their vehicle forward even faster.

CHAPTER TEN

*A*s Indy increased speed and tore off down the dirt road, the four motorcycle-mounted Nazi soldiers behind him simultaneously reached up to their helmets and pulled their goggles down over their eyes before they accelerated, too. There was a fork in the road ahead, with a smaller road that led down a hill to the left and a slightly wider road that ascended to the right.

During his journey to the castle with Elsa, Indy had studied a map of the area. He wasn't sure which fork to take, but he had to go somewhere, so he turned left down the hill. Three of the soldiers raced after him, but the fourth took the high road.

Henry nearly lost his grip on his bag when Indy weaved around a sharp corner. As Indy glanced back at the three soldiers behind him, his motorbike began to drift to the left side of the road. Henry's hand darted up to grab the right handlebar, setting the motorbike straight with a jerk, and Indy returned his gaze forward.

Indy saw a road station with two barricades up ahead. The barricades were wide, wooden gates that stretched across the road. A guard was stationed beside the first barricade, and when he saw their approach, he ran from his post and waved his arms, trying to signal them to stop. Indy ignored the guard, and Henry cringed and ducked as Indy sent the motorbike straight at the barricade.

"Halt! Halt!" the guard shouted after Indy as his motorbike and sidecar smashed through the wooden barrier. Knowing that three Nazi soldiers were still right behind him, Indy kept the bike at full speed as he headed for the second barricade. But just then, the barrier shattered at the impact of the motorcycle ridden by the fourth Nazi soldier, the one who had taken the high road — and, apparently, a short cut — so he could approach Indy from the opposite direction.

A flagpole was embedded in the ground at the side of road to Indy's left. Indy grabbed the pole as he drove past it, snapping it free from its base. While the oncoming Nazi soldier unshouldered his machine gun, Indy shifted the broken flagpole in his left arm and held it out like a lance.

There was a loud crack as the tip of the flagpole met the torso of the Nazi soldier, knocking him clear off his motorcycle. Part of the flagpole broke off, but Indy held tight to the remaining portion. Henry Jones knew all about jousting competitions from his history books, but he had never expected his own son to show such mettle.

As Henry gazed at his son with some admiration, the felled soldier's motorcycle continued to hurtle toward the first shattered barricade . . . just as the three other Nazi soldiers were racing past the guard's station. The riderless motorcycle collided with two of the soldiers, who crashed and rolled across the ground.

The one remaining Nazi soldier maneuvered his motorcycle around his fallen comrades and continued the chase. Indy saw the soldier coming up fast behind him and accelerate around a curve. Although the sidecar's weight helped stabilize Indy's motorbike, it also made his vehicle slower than his pursuer's.

The soldier twisted his motorcycle's throttle and jerked back on the handlebars, lifting his front wheel up off the road. Balancing on his rear wheel, he raced up behind Indy and dropped his front tire upon the back of the sidecar, nearly hitting Henry. Indy swerved away and the soldier's wheel slid off the sidecar and returned to the road.

Keeping both wheels on the ground, the soldier accelerated and came up fast on Indy's left. As the soldier reached for his machine gun and prepared to fire, Indy quickly extended the remaining length of the flagpole and rammed it through the spokes of the soldier's front wheel. The soldier's motorcycle flipped over the jammed wheel and somersaulted through the air before landing with a horrid crash.

Indy glanced back at the demolished bike and grinned. He thought his father would look happy, too, or at least relieved, but his father merely offered a slight grimace before removing his pocket watch from his jacket to check the time.

Facing forward, Indy saw a wooden sign at a crossroad. At the top of the sign, arrows pointed in opposite directions for Berlin and Venedig. As Indy started down the road for Venedig, Henry said, "Stop."

"What?"

"Stop! Stop!" Henry bellowed.

Indy brought the motorbike to a stop.

"You're going the wrong way," Henry said over the idling engine. "We have to get to Berlin."

Pointing toward Venedig, Indy said, "Brody's *this* way."

"My diary's in Berlin."

"We don't *need* the diary, Dad," Indy said sternly as he looked down at his father in the sidecar. "Marcus has the map!"

"There is more in the diary than just the map."

Indy turned off the engine. "All right, Dad. Tell me."

"Well," Henry said cagily, "he who finds the Grail must face the final challenge."

"What final challenge?"

Holding up three fingers, Henry said, "Three devices of such lethal cunning."

"Booby traps?"

"Oh, yes," Henry replied with glee. "But I found the clues that will safely take us through, in the Chronicles of St. Anselm."

"Well, what are they?"

Henry's lower lip quivered, and then he squinted as he lowered his gaze from Indy.

Getting angry as well as impatient, Indy said, "Can't you *remember*?"

Henry took off his hat and answered, "I wrote them down in my diary so that I wouldn't *have* to remember."

Pointing to the road behind them, Indy scowled and said, "Half the German army's on our tail, and you want me to go to Berlin? Into the lion's den?"

"Yes!" Henry said. "The only thing that matters is the Grail."

"What about Marcus?"

"Marcus would agree with me."

Looking away from his father, Indy muttered, "Two selfless martyrs." Then he returned his gaze to his father, shook his head, and exclaimed, "Jesus Christ!"

Henry slapped his son across the face. Indy gasped and his whole body shuddered. As tough as he was, he had not been prepared for his father's strike, not on any level.

"That's for blasphemy," Henry said.

Indy looked away and stared at the ground in front of the motorbike. His left cheek still stung from the slap.

In a grave tone, Henry continued, "The quest for the Grail is not archaeology. It's a race against evil. If it is captured by the Nazis, the armies of darkness will march all over the face of the Earth. Do you understand me?"

Indy's eyes burned with anger as he turned his head to face his father. Aiming a finger at Henry, he said, "This is an *obsession*, Dad. I *never* understood it. *Never*." Looking away from his father, he added, "Neither did Mom."

Henry's body stiffened in the sidecar. "Oh, yes, she did," he said. "Only too well." Lowering his voice to almost a whisper, he said, "Unfortunately, she kept her illness from me until all I could do was mourn her."

Still looking away from his father, Indy thought about his mother. Anna Jones had contracted scarlet fever and died in 1912, not long after the Jones family ended a two-year tour of the world and returned to America.

Both Indy and his father had been devastated by her loss. Unfortunately, Henry Jones had not known how to put his grief into words and had done little to console his son. Shortly after Anna's death, Henry and Indy moved to Utah, where the emotional gulf between father and son only grew.

Indy lifted his gaze to the wooden sign at the crossroad. He stared hard at the word *Berlin*, and wondered if his mother really had understood his father.

Indy restarted the motorbike and drove off with his father in the sidecar.

Night had fallen on Berlin, where the Nazis were holding a massive rally in the city square in front of the Institute of Aryan Culture, a wide Neoclassical building with a peaked roof and a façade of monolithic columns. At the center of the square, a book-burning was in progress. The Nazis were delighted to destroy any and all books that they regarded as decadent or insignificant, books that did not glorify the German people or their leader. The mound of burning books was ten feet tall and growing by the minute as college students and Nazi brownshirts tossed more books onto the fire. As the flames rose higher and martial music filled the night air, a parade of soldiers marched around the square, carrying banners that displayed the swastika.

The Nazi revelers were so absorbed by the rally that they did not notice when two men arrived by a motorbike with a sidecar, which they parked at the edge of the square. Fortunately for Indiana Jones and his father, there were so many Nazi soldiers in the vicinity that it would take them some time to discover that one was missing.

Indy had found a Nazi officer who was about his size and build. The officer had been standing alone near some parked cars when Indy knocked him out and then hastily removed the man's gray uniform and hat. After disguising himself in the Nazi uniform, Indy stuffed his own clothes and gear into his father's bag and placed them in their stolen motorbike's sidecar. Then he walked slowly over to his father, who stood silently as he watched the book-burning from a distance. Even though they were over fifty feet away from the flames, Indy could feel the heat.

"My boy," Henry said, "we are pilgrims in an unholy land."

Henry directed Indy's gaze to a podium in front of the Institute, which was decorated with enormous Nazi banners. High-ranking officers of the Third Reich stood upon the podium, and at the center was their leader, Adolf

Hitler. And just a few feet away from Hitler stood Dr. Elsa Schneider.

Despite the distance, Indy saw that Elsa appeared uncomfortable, possibly even troubled. She kept looking toward the burning books, then averting her gaze, and then looking toward the flames again. But because Elsa had betrayed him and his father, Indy could not have cared less whether she was even slightly disturbed by the sight of some books being destroyed. If things went his way, he was about to make her life a whole lot more miserable.

The Nazi rally was still going strong when Elsa left the podium. She was alone, walking past the shadows of the Institute's columns and heading back to her car, when Indy slunk out from the darkness behind her. "Fräulein Doctor." As she turned, he gripped her arm and growled, "Where is it?"

Elsa was startled by the sight of Indy. Not just because he was wearing a Nazi officer's uniform, but because he was alive at all. She gasped, "How did you get here?"

"Where is it?" Indy repeated. "I want it." He pushed her back up against a column and began to search her clothing. He found his father's diary in one of her pockets and pulled it out.

"You came back for the *book*?" Elsa said, trembling. She seemed almost disappointed, like she had hoped Indy had come all the way to Berlin for her. With a pained expression, she asked, "*Why?*"

"My father didn't want it incinerated." Indy released her and began walking away.

Realizing that Indy was referring to the book-burning that was still going on in the square, Elsa reacted as if he had slapped her. Walking fast, she stepped in front of him to stop him and said, "Is that what you think of me? I believe in the Grail, *not* the swastika."

Through clenched teeth, Indy snarled, "Yet you stood up to be counted with the enemy of everything the Grail stands for. Who cares what you think?!"

"*You* do," Elsa said quickly and desperately.

Now it was Indy's turn to feel smacked. He'd made a mistake when he'd fallen for Elsa, and he wasn't the sort of man who liked to make the same mistake twice. As sincere as she sounded, Indy knew she had a talent for faking sincerity. His left hand flew to her neck and he locked his thumb around her throat. He said, "All I have to do is squeeze."

Keeping her eyes on Indy's, Elsa answered sadly, "All I have to do is scream."

While the martial music continued to blare from the city square, Indy and Elsa just stood there for a moment, staring at each other. It was a standoff. Indy knew he wasn't capable of strangling Elsa, and she knew it, too. And the same went for screaming. There were dozens of Nazis within earshot, and even though a single scream would alert them to Indy's position, Elsa just couldn't do it.

Indy removed his hand from her neck and backed away. Elsa looked even more pained as he walked off, not because he was taking the Grail diary with him, but because she had realized that mistakes had been made. *Her* mistakes. She had failed to recognize the evils of the Nazi party, and she had never planned on falling in love with Indiana Jones.

Henry Jones was standing among a crowd of people at the bottom of a flight of steps outside the Institute. As the disguised Indy descended the steps to rejoin his father, he held the diary up and said, "I've got it. Let's get out of here."

Indy and Henry had barely taken two steps when they were suddenly thrust apart by a wave of frenzied people, all shouting and eager to catch a glimpse of the Nazi party's leader. Indy held tight to the diary but was unable to resist the force of the mob, and was shoved backwards as the crowd swept him toward the marchers in the square. When he came to a sudden stop, he turned and found himself face-to-face with Adolf Hitler.

Indy gasped as his eyes met Hitler's. He was so surprised that he almost forgot that he was wearing a Nazi officer's uniform. Hitler had been moving through the crowd with his Nazi entourage and was surrounded by numerous spectators who held out autograph books, hoping to get Hitler's signature.

Hitler's eyes flicked to the leather-bound book that Indy held in one upraised hand. Remembering that he was in disguise, Indy stopped gaping and straightened his back to stand at attention. He stood in stunned silence as Hitler reached out and took the Grail diary from him, and then took a pen from a nearby aide.

Indy held his breath as Hitler opened the diary to the first page and began to sign it. He wondered if Hitler could read English and if he might spot any mention of the Holy Grail or Henry Jones's name. But a moment later, Hitler completed his signature and handed the diary back to Indy.

Indy grinned as Hitler and his entourage moved on. As much as the Nazis had wanted to get their hands on the Grail diary, their leader had literally let it slip through his fingers.

Working his way through the crowd, Indy found his father. A Nazi S.S. officer wearing a long black overcoat spotted them as they approached the stolen motorbike and sidecar. Noticing Indy's uniform and believing him to be a Nazi soldier, the S.S. officer loudly ordered him to return to his post. Indy silenced the man with his fist and relieved him of his overcoat.

As Henry climbed into the sidecar, it did cross Indy's mind that Elsa might alert the Nazis that he and his father had recovered the diary in Berlin. He didn't know whether she would rat him out, had no reason to trust that she wouldn't, and didn't really care. If she brought more trouble, he would just have to deal with it.

CHAPTER ELEVEN

*A*fter hiding out in Berlin for the night, Indy and his father rode to the airport, where they abandoned their motorbike and sidecar. Indy also got rid of his officer's uniform, but kept the pilfered overcoat, which he put on over his own clothes before he and Henry entered the terminal building.

Inside the terminal, Nazi agents in black coats distributed leaflets bearing Henry Jones's photograph to soldiers stationed throughout the building. While Indy went to a ticket booth, Henry kept out of sight by standing beside a doorway behind some men who, like himself, were reading newspapers. Henry held his own newspaper up high so no one could see his face.

Indy turned up the collar of his overcoat and did his best to look casual as he walked past some soldiers and returned to his father. Henry tucked his newspaper under his arm as he stepped away from his hiding spot and followed Indy toward the boarding gates. Seeing the tickets in his son's hands, Henry said, "What did you get?"

"I don't know," Indy admitted. "The first available flight out of Germany."

"Good," Henry said.

They showed their tickets to the boarding guards and then got into line with a group of passengers who were moving toward a moored zeppelin. At a glance, Indy guessed the aircraft was ten stories tall and longer than two football fields. He also noticed that it had a biplane secured to its underside. Henry took a look at the tickets and informed his son that the zeppelin was bound for Athens.

They boarded the massive aircraft and made their way to a small dining table beside a wide-open louvered window in the luxurious passenger compartment. Outside the window, men were loading luggage and supplies onto the zeppelin. As Indy and Henry took their seats and Henry opened his newspaper, Indy smiled broadly and said in a hushed voice, "Well, we made it."

Lowering his paper to look at his son, Henry said, "When we're airborne, with Germany behind us, *then* I'll share that sentiment." He returned to his newspaper, holding it up so no one could see his face.

"Relax," Indy said. But then Indy looked out the

window to his left, and what he saw made him realize his father had had every reason to be concerned. Colonel Vogel and a black uniformed Gestapo agent were rushing across the tarmac, heading toward the zeppelin's gangplank.

"*Nicht zumachen!*" Vogel yelled to someone Indy couldn't see. "*Wir steigen ein!*"

They're coming aboard, Indy realized. He was about to say something to his father when a steward, an older man with gray hair who wore a white jacket and hat, stepped over and placed a bowl of nuts on their table. As the steward turned and walked down the aisle past other passengers, Indy quietly got up from his seat and followed the steward, who was a few inches shorter than him. When Indy caught up with the steward in the foyer outside the passenger compartment, he put his arm around the man's shoulder and addressed him in a low, confidential tone as he led him up a flight of stairs.

A moment after Indy left with the steward, Vogel entered the passenger compartment. Vogel carried a walking stick, and as he moved down the aisle, he raised the stick to push down at the top of a newspaper that had been obscuring a male passenger's face. There were three other people seated at the table with the man, and they all looked up at Vogel as he held up a photograph of Henry Jones and said, "*Haben sie disen Mann gesehen?*"

The passengers did not recognize the man in the photo. They shook their heads and said, "*Nein.*"

While the zeppelin remained moored, Vogel moved on to another group of passengers, from whom he received the same response. As he noticed yet another person concealed behind a raised newspaper, Indy emerged from a nearby doorway. Indy was wearing the white jacket and hat that he had just appropriated from the steward. The hat fit well enough, but the jacket was more than a little snug. Indy saw Vogel, turned to face a seated passenger, and asked the passenger for his ticket: "*Fahrscheine, bitte.*"

The passenger answered, "*Ich habe ihn nicht gesehen.*"

With mounting tension, Indy watched Vogel move toward the table where Henry was concealed behind his newspaper. Indy stepped over to the seated passengers that Vogel had just left and said in a low voice, "Tickets, please." Only when no one responded did he realize that he'd spoken in English. He glanced down to a female passenger and said, "*Fahrscheine meine Dame. Bitte.*"

As the passengers beside Indy slowly reached for their tickets, Vogel slowly brought his walking stick down on top of the newspaper in Henry's hands. Henry looked at the tip of the walking stick, then lifted his gaze to Vogel.

Henry had removed his spectacles. He squinted at the man who had interrupted his reading and then went suddenly tense when he realized who it was. Vogel smiled menacingly and said, "*Guten Tag, Herr Jones.*"

Indy moved behind Vogel and said, "*Fahrscheine meine Herr.*"

Keeping his eyes fixed on Henry, Vogel said over his shoulder, "*Weg.*"

Indy said, "Tickets, please."

Henry squinted at the steward who stood behind Vogel. Henry wondered if something were wrong with his hearing. He could have sworn the steward sounded just like his own son.

With mild annoyance, Vogel said, "*Was?*" He turned to face the white-jacketed man behind him. And then he recognized Indy.

Indy threw his right fist into Vogel's jaw. Vogel stumbled past Henry's table and fell against the sill of the open window. As frightened passengers gasped and recoiled, Indy grabbed the back of Vogel's jacket and belt and heaved him out of the zeppelin. Vogel fell over twenty feet before he crashed down upon a large pile of luggage.

The fight had happened so fast, most of the shocked passengers blinked in bewilderment as Indy stepped away from the open window. Indy faced the gawking passengers and aimed a thumb at the open window. "No ticket."

All of the passengers gaped at Indy for a second, and then there was a sudden flurry of activity as hands dipped quickly into pockets and purses to produce tickets. A moment later, everyone was holding up their tickets for Indy to see.

Below the zeppelin, Vogel crawled out from the pile of luggage just as the massive aircraft began to rise into the sky. Standing amidst the luggage, he shook his fist and shouted, "*Du wirst nochmal boren von mir!*"

Indy had slipped out of the steward's white jacket and hat and back into his own clothes. Indy wasn't too concerned that the crew would figure out an SS officer had been thrown overboard because, while no one had been looking, he had disabled the zeppelin's radio. Later, as the airship traveled over a mountain range, he couldn't help looking a bit smug while he had a drink with his father in the passenger compartment's dining lounge.

Henry was cleaning his spectacles with a handkerchief when he looked across the small table to Indy, who was wearing his leather jacket. Henry said, "You know, sharing your adventures is an interesting experience."

Henry's Grail diary was on the table. As he opened the diary and began flipping through the pages, Indy said, "Do you remember the last time we had a quiet drink? I had a milkshake."

"Hmm?" Henry said without looking up from his diary. "What did we talk about?"

"We didn't talk," Indy said, staring down at the drink in front of him. "We never talked."

A moment later, Henry said, "Do I detect a rebuke?"

"A regret," Indy admitted. "It was just the two of us, Dad. It was a lonely way to grow up. For you, too. If you had been an ordinary, average father like the other guys' dads, you'd have understood that."

Still looking at his diary, Henry shook his head and smiled. "Actually, I was a wonderful father."

"When?"

Henry's brow furrowed as he lifted his gaze to his son. "Did I ever tell you to eat up?" he said sharply. "Go to bed? Wash your ears? Do your homework? No. I respected your privacy, and I taught you self-reliance."

Indy leaned forward with his elbows braced upon the table. "What you taught me was that I was less important to you than people who'd been dead for five hundred years in another country," he said bitterly. "And I learned it so well that we've hardly spoken for twenty years."

"You *left*," Henry said emphatically, "just when you were becoming *interesting*."

"Unbelievable," Indy muttered as he rocked back in his chair. "Dad, how can you —?"

"Very well," Henry interrupted. "I'm here. Now ..." He closed his journal and sat erect, staring at Indy. "What do you want to talk about? Hmm?"

"Well, I ..." Indy exhaled, flustered. "Uh ..." He glanced away from his father, and then looked back. Henry just sat there staring at him. Indy shook his head and laughed. "I can't think of anything."

Holding his arms out at his sides, Henry exclaimed, "Then what are you *complaining* about? Look, we have *work* to do!" Holding the back of his chair, he made a series of small hops to shift his chair over closer to Indy. Then he opened his diary again so Indy could see the pages he had been reading, and said, "When we get to Alexandretta, we will face three challenges. The first, 'The Breath of God, only the penitent man will pass.'"

Indy got out his own eyeglasses, put them on, and saw his father was reciting handwritten notes. Henry had also drawn a picture of the Holy Grail, an undecorated goblet with lines radiating out around it. Beneath the drawing, Henry had written, *The cup of a carpenter*.

"Second," Henry continued, "'The Word of God, only in the footsteps of God will he proceed.' Third, 'The Path of God, only in the leap from the lion's head will he prove his worth.'"

Indy read the words to himself as Henry said them aloud, but then he looked at his father with a blank expression and asked, "What does that *mean*?"

Henry shrugged and chuckled. "I don't know." Then he nudged his son and added gleefully, "We'll find out!"

Indy smiled, too. But a moment later, as he removed his eyeglasses, he noticed that the shadows cast by the drinking glasses on their table had begun to move counterclockwise, and then he heard the zeppelin's engines whine. As the sunlight pouring in through the compartment's windows shifted suddenly across the walls, Indy looked up and said with grim certainty, "We're turning around. They're taking us back to Germany."

Mere minutes after the zeppelin had swung around over the mountain and began heading back to Berlin, Indy and his father snuck into the belly of the zeppelin, where the aircraft's elaborate metal framework was exposed. Indy carried his father's umbrella and leather bag, and both men had their hats on. Although Indy had no intention of starting a gunfight inside the highly-flammable zeppelin, he had taken the precaution of sticking his revolver down into his belt.

As Indy led his father down an aluminum ladder to a long, narrow catwalk, he grumbled, "Well, I thought it would take them a lot longer to figure out the radio was dead. Come on, Dad. Move!"

Their shoes made clacking sounds as they ran the length of the catwalk until they arrived at an open hatch in the floor. A ladder went down the hatch. As Indy began scampering down the ladder, he shouted, "Come on, Dad. Come on!"

They felt a great rush of wind as they went down the ladder, for it descended out of the zeppelin and into the open air, straight into the open cockpit of the biplane that was suspended from the zeppelin by a hook and crane device. Right behind the pilot's seat was a mounted machine gun. As Indy lowered himself behind the pilot's controls and his father climbed into the tail gunner's seat, Henry slapped the back of Indy's leather jacket and said with delight, "I didn't know you could fly a plane!"

"Fly — yes!" Indy said, shouting over the wind, but quickly added, "Land — no!" He started the biplane's engine and released the mechanism that secured it to the zeppelin. A moment later, the biplane fell from the zeppelin's belly, and Indy and his father were flying across the great blue sky. Indy didn't know exactly where they were, but he knew they were over Turkey, not far from the Mediterranean coast.

As the zeppelin receded into the distance, Indy turned around to see his father grinning as he gazed down at the ground below. Elsa had been wrong about a lot of things, but Indy figured she had made at least one good call: his father really *did* look as giddy as a schoolboy sometimes. *A big, old, bearded schoolboy*, Indy thought with some amusement.

Indy smiled at his father and gave him the thumbs-up signal. Henry smiled back, but then they both became aware of a strange sound in the skies behind them, a sound that was a cross between a roar and a wail. Both men gazed past the biplane's rear stabilizer to see two fighter planes racing toward them. The planes were painted with German Air Force colors.

One of the Nazi fighters opened fire on the biplane. A moment later, the fighter screamed past the biplane and began circling back. Indy knew there was no way he could outrun the Nazi fighters, and he severely doubted he could outmaneuver them, at least not at their current altitude. As he guided the biplane into a dive, he shouted back, "Dad, you're gonna have to use the machine gun! Get it ready!"

Henry wore a perplexed expression as he turned and gripped the machine gun.

"Eleven o'clock!" Indy shouted as he aimed his left arm toward the upper left area of the sky in front of the biplane. "Dad, eleven o'clock!"

Henry took his hands off the machine gun and removed his pocket watch from his jacket. After examining his watch, he put it back in his pocket and turned around to his son. "What happens at eleven o'clock?"

Frustrated beyond belief, and thinking he would have been better off with an *actual* schoolboy in the gunner's seat, Indy raised his left arm again to demonstrate that he was referring to a direction and not a time. He chopped at the air, moving his arm counter-clockwise as he shouted "Twelve, eleven, ten!" Then he pointed at the incoming fighter and shouted, "Eleven o'clock! Fire!"

Henry got the idea. He swung the machine gun around and fired high and to the left over the biplane's upper wing, aiming for the speeding fighter. The machine gun shuddered in his hands with such violence that he was afraid he'd be shaken out of his seat, but he held tight to the trigger and continued firing at the fighter as it whizzed past the biplane.

Indy was amazed that they hadn't taken even one hit, and then he realized that the biplane's slow speed and small size were actually working to their advantage. The Nazi fighters flew *so* fast that they continually overshot the biplane and then were forced to make wide turns before they could take aim again. Indy knew his only chance was to fly even lower, close over the hills and trees below, where the fighter planes would be even less maneuverable.

As Indy guided the biplane down over a small forest, Henry took aim at one of the fighters and opened fire. The fighter banked hard to the left, but Henry swung the machine gun around, kept the fighter in his sights, and continued firing. He kept firing as the fighter tore off and away from the biplane, but failed to hold his fire as his machine gun swung toward the biplane's rear stabilizer. An instant later, Henry had inadvertently blasted through the stabilizer, completely destroying it.

Indy had not seen his father's accidental action, but he knew something bad had happened by the way the biplane suddenly dropped altitude. As Henry gaped at the ruined stabilizer, Indy shouted over his shoulder, "Dad, are we hit?"

"More or less," Henry replied. "Son, I'm sorry."

As Indy turned his head to see the missing tail section, his father added, "They got us."

The biplane's engine sputtered, and then it began to go down.

CHAPTER TWELVE

Indy struggled with the biplane's controls, trying to slow its descent. "Hang on, Dad!" he shouted. "We're going in!"

The terrain was mountainous. Henry saw they were descending toward a shrub-covered hill. He fearfully ducked and braced himself in the gunner's seat. A moment later, the biplane's wheels crashed down on the ground, sending the plane skidding out of control toward a rickety corral of goats. A cloud of dust trailed behind the biplane as Indy tried to kill the dying engine. As he neared the corral, the goats panicked and stampeded through a wooden fence. A moment later, both the biplane and its propeller came to a sudden stop when it slammed into the side of the adjacent barn.

"Nice landing," Henry said sarcastically.

"Thanks," Indy said as he pulled himself out of the cockpit, taking his father's bag and umbrella with him. Henry scrambled out after his son.

The Nazi pilots sighted the crashed biplane and swooped down toward the farm. Indy and Henry heard the fighters coming and ran away from the barn and across an open field. One of the fighters opened fire, and bullets slammed into the ground behind the running men.

There was a low retaining wall at the edge of the field, and Henry and Indy jumped down to hug the side of the wall as the fighter soared over their position. Outraged, Henry gasped, "Those people are trying to kill us!"

"I *know*, Dad!" Indy roared.

"Well," Henry said meekly. "It's a new experience for me."

"It happens to me all the time," Indy said. He shoved the bag and umbrella into his father's arms, and then ran from the retaining wall. Henry followed.

Nearby, alongside a gravel road, an old man was repairing one of the rear tires of his car, a Citröen Traction Avant convertible. The old man was about to place a hubcap over the jacked-up rear wheel when he heard two planes whine overhead. After he watched the fighters pass, he picked up the hubcap and moved it into position beside the wheel. But before he could set the hubcap in place, his car's engine started and the entire vehicle rolled away, right off the jacks.

In the car's passenger seat, Henry looked nervous as Indy gripped the steering wheel and stomped on the accelerator. Henry didn't like the fact that they'd just stolen an old man's car, but he liked the idea of getting shot down by Nazi fighters even less. Indy was just glad that the car had front-wheel drive, or their getaway wouldn't have been nearly so easy.

Then Indy glanced to the car's side mirror and saw the reflection of one of the fighters. It was flying low, coming up fast behind them. As Indy sent the car faster down the mountain road, the fighter's pilot opened fire, sending twin streams of bullets into the road behind the stolen Citröen.

"This is intolerable!" Henry cried.

Indy saw the road curve up ahead and said, "This could be close."

Indy took the curve fast and drove straight into a tunnel that cut through the steep mountainside. A moment after the car entered the tunnel, the low-flying fighter wrapped around the curve. The pilot was unable to pull up in time, and his fighter slammed into the mouth of the tunnel. The wings sheared off at the impact, but the fuselage continued to rocket through the tunnel like a bullet down the muzzle of a gun. Sparks flew as its belly scraped against the pavement and the tunnel's rough-hewn sides.

Indy and Henry glanced back over their shoulders to see that the wingless fuselage had been transformed into a racing fireball. Even worse, the fuselage had maintained its velocity and was rapidly gaining on them.

Glancing at his son, Henry urged, "Faster, boy! Faster!"

But Indy couldn't go any faster, not without losing control of the car. Maintaining speed, he steered the car so that he was traveling as close as he dared along the right wall of the cave. A moment later, the flaming fuselage cruised past the left side of the Citröen, so close that Indy and Henry could see the stunned German pilot gaping at them before he hurtled ahead.

As the fuselage exited the cave, it exploded in all directions. Indy and Henry ducked their heads as they made their own exit and drove straight through the wall of flames and over the scattered debris that covered the road. Indy held tight to the wheel, and when Henry looked back, he was amazed to see they had cleared the burning wreckage.

"Well," Henry chuckled, "they don't come much closer than that!"

At that very moment, the remaining fighter plane released a bomb that fell to the road directly in front of the Citröen. The bomb exploded, missing the car by only several feet and instantly creating a deep, wide crater in the road. Indy was unable to stop the car from nosing straight into it.

Dust and dirt were everywhere. Indy scrambled out of the car and bounded up to the side of the road, which overlooked a steep hill that stretched down to the

Mediterranean Sea. Glancing around, Indy saw they were completely exposed. Henry had already extricated himself from the car, but Indy turned and gestured at the fighter as he said impatiently, "Dad, he's coming back."

Clutching his bag and umbrella, Henry trotted off after Indy and followed him down the hill, which led to a wide beach. Indy had hoped to find some kind of protective cover along the beach, but except for some distant rocks, there was nothing.

Overhead, the Nazi fighter began to circle back toward them.

Indy remembered his revolver and pulled it from his belt. Had anyone ever used a handgun to shoot a fighter plane out of the sky? Indy had no idea, but he would give it his best shot.

But then Indy remembered something else. He opened the revolver's chamber and saw it was empty. In all the excitement, he'd forgotten to load his gun.

We're dead.

While Indy just stood there, Henry gazed down the stretch of beach between them and the approaching fighter. Without a word, he thrust his leather bag into Indy's arms and then drew his umbrella out from straps at the top of the bag. Indy noticed that his father had removed the umbrella with a slight flourish, like a knight unsheathing his sword.

Then, even more unexpectedly, Henry left Indy's side and began running down the beach. As he ran, he made clucking noises as he rapidly opened and closed his umbrella. Only then did Indy notice that his father was heading for a large flock of seagulls that had gathered along the shore.

At Henry's approach, the seagulls became agitated and took to the wing. Indy watched with wonderment as thousands of birds suddenly rose up into the sky, just as the fighter swooped down from above.

Before the pilot could take evasive action, his fighter collided with the unfortunate birds. Some gulls were shredded by the whirling propeller blades. Others smashed straight into the cockpit with such impact that they cracked the glass. The pilot screamed as he fired blind into the sky. A moment later, his out-of-control fighter slammed into a high rocky wall that loomed above the beach.

Slightly stunned, Indy pocketed his revolver and turned to see his father walking back up the beach. Henry casually held his open umbrella over his shoulder, shielding his face from the sun. As he returned to his son's side, Henry said, "I suddenly remembered my Charlemagne. 'Let my armies be the rocks and the trees and the birds in the sky.'" Then, like a schoolboy, Henry chuckled.

Indy knew that if it hadn't been for Henry's quick

thinking and action, both of them probably would have been shot dead. As Henry walked past him, Indy felt slightly ashamed that he had been treating his father like excess baggage. He also felt something else for his father that he hadn't before: pride.

In the Republic of Hatay, a Sultan received a group of visitors to his palace in Iskenderun. The Sultan wore a red fez and an ornate gold tunic. His visitors included Walter Donovan, Colonel Vogel, a few Nazi soldiers, and the captive, Marcus Brody.

In a palace courtyard, Donovan and Vogel walked alongside the Sultan, followed by Brody, an armed Nazi soldier, some Turkish soldiers, and the Sultan's various minions. Donovan clutched the Grail diary's missing pages, and Brody couldn't help but wince at the sight. As they walked, Donovan held the pages out before the Sultan and said, "These pages are taken from Professor Jones's diary, Your Highness. And they include a map that pinpoints the exact location of the Grail. As you can see, the Grail is all but in our hands."

The Sultan gave the map a cursory glance, but showed no real interest in it.

"However, Your Highness," Donovan continued, "we would not think of crossing your soil without your permission, nor of removing the Grail from your borders without suitable compensation."

The Sultan stopped walking, and everyone else stopped, too. Glancing at Donovan, the Sultan got straight to the point and said, "What have you brought?"

In response, Vogel looked over to two nearby Nazi soldiers and snapped, "Bring *den Schatz!*"

The two soldiers brought forward a large steamer trunk. They placed it on the ground in front of the Sultan and then pulled its lid open. The trunk was filled with gold and silver objects of every description. Vogel dipped his walking stick into the trunk to lift a gold pitcher for the Sultan's inspection.

"Precious valuables, Your Highness," Donovan said, "donated by some of the finest families in all of Germany."

But Donovan had lost the Sultan before he'd even said the word "donated." Apparently, the Sultan had little use for these expensive trinkets, for he stepped away from Donovan and the offered treasure and moved to the center of the courtyard, where he'd seen something else that had taken his fancy.

"Ah!" exclaimed the Sultan as he opened his arms to the gleaming black Nazi staff car that had delivered the foreigners to his palace. "Rolls-Royce Phantom Two," the Sultan declared. Then, glancing at Donovan while he made sweeping gestures at the car, the Sultan rattled off the car's specifications from memory. "Four-point-three liter, thirty horsepower, six cylinder engine, with Stromberg downdraft carburetor. Can go from zero to one hundred kilometers an hour in twelve-point-five seconds. And I even like the color."

Donovan smiled as he removed his hat with an almost bowing gesture and said, "The keys are in the ignition, Your Highness."

Stepping away from the Rolls-Royce, the Sultan said, "You shall have camels, horses, an armed escort, provisions, desert vehicles — and tanks!"

"You're welcome," Donovan said.

The Sultan led Donovan and Vogel past a man who happened to be a spy at the palace. Like the Sultan, the man wore a red fez. As Donovan and Vogel passed him, the spy turned his head and eyed them carefully. The spy was Kazim, agent of the Brotherhood of the Cruciform Sword.

A short while later, after completing their negotiations with the Sultan, Donovan and Vogel were walking through a corridor at the palace when they saw a blonde woman wearing a trim dress suit and sunhat coming down a stairway.

"We have no time to lose," Dr. Elsa Schneider said as she approached the two men. "Indiana Jones and his father have escaped."

CHAPTER THIRTEEN

*I*ndy and Henry wasted no time traveling to Iskenderun. There, they were greeted by Sallah, who led them to an open car. Indy climbed into the front seat beside Sallah, and Henry got in back. As Sallah drove them through the crowded streets, he explained how Marcus Brody had been abducted by the Nazis. Listening to Sallah's account, Indy and Henry scowled.

There were many pedestrians, carpet sellers, and goats in the street. "We go this way," Sallah said as he blasted the car's horn and weaved through the crowd. Steering onto a narrow street, they came up fast behind a man herding three camels. Sallah hit his horn again and shouted, "Get that camel out of the way!"

Indy said, "What happened to Marcus, Sallah?"

"Ah, they set out across the desert this afternoon. I believe they took Mister Brody with them."

Henry removed his hat and whacked the back of Indy's

jacket with it. "Now they have the map!" Henry said angrily. Leaning forward from the backseat, he added, "And in this sort of race, there's no silver medal for finishing second."

The Sultan had supplied Donovan with all he needed for an expedition across the rocky desert: staff cars, troop carriers, supply trucks, riding camels, spare horses, and Turkish soldiers to serve alongside their German counterparts. As promised, he had also let them borrow his prized tank, a modified British type from the Great War. Equipped with a large turret-mounted primary cannon and two side cannons, the thirty-six-feet long treaded tank was a massive war machine. It was operated by a driver and side gunner, who had been instructed to obey Colonel Vogel's commands. Vogel was proud to have the tank lead Donovan's procession across the rocky desert.

To allow those on foot to keep up, the drivers kept their vehicles at a relatively low speed as they moved along through the ramble of a box canyon. In the front seat of an open car directly behind the tank, Donovan, wearing a pith helmet and a tailored safari jacket, sat beside the driver. In the back seat were Elsa and Brody. Elsa wore a white shirt with black pants and matching black gloves and leather boots; she had pushed her hair up under a German soldier's cap and wore field goggles to keep the dust out of her eyes. Brody wore the same suit he'd been wearing since his arrival and abduction in Iskenderun; he looked rumpled, exhausted, and miserable.

Donovan handed a canteen back to Brody and said, "Care to wet your whistle, Marcus?"

"I'd rather spit in your face," Brody replied. "But as I haven't got any spit . . ." He took the canteen, but before he could open it and raise it to his parched lips, Vogel walked up alongside the moving car, stepped on its running board, and plucked the canteen from Brody's hands.

Holding the canteen, Vogel stepped down from the running board and continued to walk beside the vehicle. As he opened the canteen, he said to Donovan, "Must be within three or four miles. Otherwise we are off the map." Vogel handed the pages torn from the Grail diary to Elsa and then drank from the canteen.

Brody glanced at the pages in Elsa's hand. She was studying the map that Henry Jones had made. Knowing that he had allowed the Nazis to take possession of the map made Brody feel ill.

Donovan removed his pith helmet and said, "Well, Marcus, we are on the brink of the recovery of the greatest artifact in the history of mankind."

As Donovan took the canteen from Vogel and raised it to his own lips, Brody said, "You're meddling with powers you cannot possibly comprehend."

"Ah," Indy said. "I see Brody. He seems okay."

Indy was stretched out on the ground, peering through binoculars from atop a high, rocky hill that overlooked Donovan's caravan. Because of the distance, he did not recognize Elsa as the goggled person who sat beside Brody in the open car.

Henry and Sallah had crouched down behind some boulders a short distance behind Indy. Beyond the boulders was a dirt road, where Sallah had parked their supply-laden car.

Indy pushed himself up from the ground and stood upright before the boulders. "They've got a tank," he said as he readjusted his binoculars. Looking at the tank's main cannon, he commented, "Six-pound gun."

Unfortunately, the bright sunlight reflected off of Indy's binoculars. In the canyon below, Donovan glanced up from his car to see a bright light flash in the upper hills.

From his hiding place behind a boulder, Henry glared at Indy and said in a loud whisper. "What do you think you're doing?! Get down!"

Turning to face his father, Indy said with some annoyance, "Dad, we're *well* out of range."

Indy's sentence was punctuated by a loud blast from the canyon floor. Indy cringed as he glanced back to see a large puff of smoke in front of the tank's main cannon and heard the fired shell tear through the air in his direction. As the shell whistled overhead, Indy dove down beside the nearby boulders, and both Henry and Sallah moved fast to take cover beside him. A split second later, the shell smashed into their parked car, blowing it to smithereens.

The three men covered their heads as automobile fragments rained down upon them. A flaming tire bounced and rolled away from the explosion. As the tire blazed past Sallah he gasped, "That car belonged to my brother-in-law."

Crouching low, Indy gestured at his father and Sallah to follow him and shouted, "Come on, come on!"

Down in the canyon, beside the tank, Vogel peered through binoculars to confirm that the fired shell had destroyed an automobile. Lowering his binoculars, he walked over to Donovan's car and said, "I can't see anyone up there."

Donovan said, "Maybe it wasn't even Jones."

"No," Elsa said. "It's him all right." She stood up in the back of the car, glanced at the surrounding hills and added, "He's here somewhere."

Donovan stepped out of the car and looked to Vogel. "Put Brody in the tank."

While Vogel escorted Brody to the tank, Donovan's party was unaware that they were surrounded by white-robed men who had concealed themselves in the hills around their position. The men were agents of the Brotherhood of the Cruciform Sword, and Kazim was among them. From his hiding place behind a rock, Kazim readied his rifle as he peered at the group below.

Elsa stepped away from Donovan's car and walked over to stand beside Donovan. While Elsa reached up to massage the back of her travel-weary neck, Donovan said, "Well, in this sun, without transportation, they're as good as dead."

Suddenly, the concealed Brotherhood opened fire on the soldiers and vehicles below. A Nazi soldier fell from the top of the tank as bullets hammered into the vehicle's armor. Elsa and Donovan ran and dived for cover beside Donovan's car. Donovan muttered, "It's Jones, all right."

But Indy was as surprised by all the gunfire as Donovan. Indy was leading his father and Sallah down the hill to the tank and parked vehicles when shots rang out from all around them. Indy and Sallah ducked down behind some rocks, but Henry stood straight up, gestured at the men in white robes who were shooting at the Nazi and Turkish soldiers, and exclaimed, "Now, who are all *these* people?"

"Who cares?" Indy said as he pulled his father down beside him. "As long as they're keeping Donovan busy." Seeing that his father looked winded, he said, "Dad, you stay here while Sallah and I organize some transportation."

Indy and Sallah snuck off, leaving Henry behind, sitting on a rock. Henry was brushing the dust from his jacket when a bullet hit the other side of the rock he was sitting on. He ducked down fast.

Donovan's party responded to their attackers with a vengeance. While two Nazi soldiers threw hand grenades into the cliffs, others opened fire with machine guns. The grenades exploded, launching dirt and white-robed men into the air. One of the men was killed instantly, and after his body rolled to a stop, a Nazi soldier bent down to see the man's exposed sternum bore a tattoo of a cruciform sword.

Indy and Sallah crouched down behind a wide rock and watched men on both sides of the battle run amongst the camels and horses. Indy said, "I'm going after those horses."

"I'll take the camels," Sallah said.

Staring hard at Sallah, Indy said, "I don't need camels."

"But, Indy —"

"No camels!" Indy insisted.

Indy moved off, heading for a hill just beyond the horses. He saw several dead men on the ground, but had no idea that Kazim had participated in the attack on Donovan's party, or that Kazim had been mortally wounded.

Kazim lay on the ground, face-up with his arms stretched out by his sides. Lifting his head slightly, he looked up to see Elsa staring down at him with a sad expression. Donovan stepped over beside Elsa, looked at the dying man before him, and said to Elsa, "Who is he?"

"A messenger from God," Kazim gasped. "For the unrighteous, the Cup of Life holds everlasting damnation."

Hearing this, Elsa trembled. Donovan glanced at her, sneered, and walked away. Elsa wondered whether Donovan held disdain for the man's words or her reaction to them, but realized it didn't matter. A moment later, as Elsa watched, Kazim lowered his head and died.

A moment after Kazim drew his last breath, Indy leaped from the hillside to tackle a mounted soldier. The soldier went down along with his horse. Indy belted the soldier as he scrambled onto the horse's saddle, and then grabbed the reins to urge the horse up from the ground. As the horse got up with Indy on its back, another soldier came running at Indy. Indy backhanded the man and galloped off.

Indy had assumed that his father would stay put and did not see Henry leave his hiding place and head for the tank. Henry had seen the Nazis put Brody inside the tank, and he was hoping to be of some aid to his old friend. He snuck up to the tank and climbed on top of it, discovering that its hatch was open.

There were just a few metal steps that led down into the tank's hatch. Henry stepped down them and found Brody seated inside the tank. Brody had his back to the hatch and looked more miserable than ever. The tank's goggled driver and side gunner were peering out through the front viewing port, and did not hear Henry's entrance.

Henry reached out and tapped Brody's shoulder as he said in loud whisper, "Marcus!"

"Arghhh!" Brody nearly jumped out of his skin. Turning around, he saw Henry crouched below the hatch and exclaimed, "Oh!"

The two men launched into the traditional University Club toast by swinging their arms at one another and deliberately missing. Then Henry flapped his arms and tugged his ears and recited, "'Genius of the Restoration —'"

Brody tugged his ears, flapped his arms, and touched his head as he responded, "'— aid our own resuscitation!'"

Then they shook hands and Brody said, "Henry! What are you doing here?"

"It's a rescue, old boy! Come on." Henry was about to get up when shadows appeared above the hatch, and then two Nazi soldiers came down fast into the tank, their Luger pistols drawn. One soldier grabbed Henry and held his gun to his head while the other aimed his own gun at Brody. Then a third Nazi stepped down into the tank. It was Vogel.

"Search him," said Vogel, his icy-blue eyes boring in on Henry's. As the soldier patted down Henry's pockets, Vogel reached to his own right hand and removed his leather glove. "What is in this book?" he said. "That miserable little diary of yours."

Before Henry could even think to respond, Vogel slapped his glove across Henry's face. Henry's head jerked to the side, and he reached up to touch his wounded cheek.

"We have the map," Vogel continued. "The book is useless, and yet you come all the way back to Berlin to get it. Why?" He slapped Henry again, and again Henry's head jerked aside.

"What are you hiding?" Vogel said. "What does the diary tell you that it doesn't tell us?!" He was about to slap Henry again when Henry, despite the pistol aimed at his head, reached up fast to catch and stop Vogel's wrist.

Barely restraining his rage, Henry growled, "It tells me that goose-stepping morons like yourself should try reading books instead of burning them!" He shoved Vogel's hand away.

Vogel's face went red with anger. Before he could strike Henry again, Donovan poked his head over the hatch and shouted down, "Colonel? Jones is getting away!"

Gesturing to Henry Jones, Vogel replied, "I think not, Herr Donovan."

"Not that Jones, the other Jones!" Donovan shouted as he gestured away from the tank and pointed to Indy.

Indy was mounted on one horse and was holding tight to the reins of three others, leading them away from the tank and soldiers. Vogel raised his head up through the hatch just in time to see the back of Indy's fedora and leather jacket as he rode off with the horses. Seething with fury, Vogel pushed his hand past Donovan to grab the inner handle on the hatch's lid, then pulled the lid shut.

Indy brought the horses around a bend in the canyon, where he caught up with Sallah, who was also mounted on a horse. But much to Indy's dismay, Sallah had acquired not more horses but the beasts that Indy had forbidden.

"Sallah, I said no camels!" Indy shouted. "That's five camels. Can't you count?!"

"Compensation for my brother-in-law's car," Sallah said defensively. "Indy, your father and Brody —"

Instantly losing all interest in the camels, Indy said, "Where's my father?"

"They have them," Sallah said, tilting his head back in the direction he and Indy had come from. "In the belly of that steel beast."

Indy clenched his jaw and looked away from Sallah. Already, he could hear the sound of the approaching tank. He gazed forward, shouted, "Hyah!" and then charged off with the horses in one direction while Sallah took off with the camels in another.

The tank, Donovan's car, and supply trucks followed Indy and Sallah around the bend in the canyon. Inside the tank, Vogel peered out through a slot, saw his quarry with the horses, and directed the tank's driver to go after Indiana Jones.

But as the tank headed off after Indy, Donovan instructed his driver to take him and Elsa in a different direction. As they veered away from the caravan, Elsa once again examined the map from Henry's diary.

The moment Indy realized that the tank and other vehicles had focused on him and not Sallah, he cut the other horses loose and rode off. As he headed for some rocky dunes, the tank increased speed and raced after him.

"Fire!" Vogel commanded the tank's driver and side gunner. Before Indy could reach the cover of the dunes, the tank fired and the nearest dune exploded into a high plume of desert dust. Indy guided his horse fast to the left and toward another dune, but then the tank fired again and it exploded, too. Inside the tank, Henry and Brody held their hands over their ears and watched helplessly as the emptied artillery shells fell to the floor.

Indy knew he had to keep the horse moving. Moving away from the dunes, he zigged and zagged over a wide-open area, forcing the tank to keep changing direction and preventing its crew from getting a bead on him. Glancing back over his shoulder, he saw the other vehicles emerge from around the dunes, and then he looked at the tank. He noticed that the tank's armored ports allowed limited visibility for the driver and that the side guns could only pivot so far, and saw an opportunity for action.

Indy guided his horse in front of the tank and then made a rapid 180 degree turn. As expected, the tank followed. But as the tank completed its full wrap-around turn, Vogel peered through the viewing port to see the oncoming German caravan. Indy had herded the tank into a head-on collision with a Kubelwagon, a German military sedan, and there was no way to avoid it.

Vogel screamed, and then the Kubelwagon smashed into the front of the tank. Everyone inside the tank was slammed against the hard-metal interior. The Kubelwagon flipped over and the tank's six-pound cannon drove straight through the sedan's roof. The force of the impact made the tank rock back on its treads, but it kept moving with the Kubelwagon now affixed over and in front of the turret, blocking not only the tank's front viewing ports but the use of its main cannon.

Still riding at full gallop, Indy shot a glance toward the tank to see that his maneuver had worked even better than expected. He laughed and then rode on ahead of the impaired tank.

One of the tank's side cannons fired. Indy was keeping his horse out of range, and the shell exploded into a dune over forty feet behind him. As he galloped onward, he saw a stone on the ground, slightly larger than a baseball. Clutching the reigns with his left hand, he leaned out from his saddle and stretched out his right arm to scoop up the stone. The horse never even broke its stride.

Incredibly, not all of the Kubelwagon's occupants had died when it collided with the tank. But as the survivors struggled to free themselves from their inverted, ruptured vehicle, Vogel decided that killing Indiana Jones was a higher priority than liberating the trapped Nazis. Turning to the gunner, Vogel ordered, "*Der Kubelwagon sprengen!*"

The gunner put a shell into the large gun and then fired, blasting the Kubelwagon straight off of the tank. The Kubelwagon sailed through the air and crashed in front of the tank. The tank never stopped moving, but drove through the smoke and dust and rolled over the Kubelwagon, crushing it.

As the tank left the flattened sedan behind, Indy guided his horse up along the left side of the tank. He held out the stone that he'd plucked from the ground, and then jammed it down the barrel of the side cannon. When the rock was firmly lodged, he rode away from the tank, steering his horse directly in range of that cannon.

Inside the tank, Henry moved over beside one of the viewing ports and peered out. One of the Nazi soldiers shoved him aside and snapped, "*Keine Bewegung.*"

Henry stumbled back and landed on a bare metal bench beside Brody. The soldier aimed his Luger pistol at them and repeated, "*Keine Bewegung.*"

The tank's side gunner had moved behind the trigger of the tank's left side cannon when he sighted Indy. The gunner grinned as he took aim and fired, but the cannon, blocked by the stone, backfired, killing the gunner instantly and filling the tank with smoke. Henry, Brody, and the Nazi soldiers began to choke and cough.

Indy saw smoke pouring out through the tank's ports. He guided his horse back alongside the tank so he was a short distance from the ruined cannon, which appeared to have blossomed into a flower of twisted metal. Turning his head to face the tank, Indy shouted, "Dad! Dad! Dad!"

Despite the noise inside the rumbling tank and that Henry's ears were still ringing from the cannon backfire, Henry heard his son's cry. The soldier who had shoved Henry away from the port still had his Luger out, but Henry shouted in return, "Junior! Junior! Junior!"

Incensed by Henry's shouting, the soldier lashed out with his gun hand, punching Henry in the jaw. Henry rocked back on the bench and glared at the soldier.

Indy had maneuvered his horse back behind the tank when Vogel popped open the hatch above the turret, releasing the smoke from within. Vogel coughed and felt his eyes tearing as the smoke billowed out and around him. And then he turned his head and saw Indy, and he reached for his pistol.

Indy knew that it was no easy trick to shoot from horseback at full gallop, but he'd had some experience. He drew his own revolver, took aim at Vogel, and fired. There was a bright flash as the bullet ricocheted off the turret, causing Vogel to duck, but Vogel quickly returned fire. The bullet tore past Indy, who kept his gun arm steady and fired more rounds at the turret.

Realizing that Indy was a much better shot and fearing for his life, Vogel ducked back down into the turret. Just as Vogel ducked, Indy tried to squeeze off another shot and was disappointed when his revolver's hammer only produced a loud *click*.

Indy jammed his revolver back down into his belt. As he kept after the tank, he thought, *How am I going to stop that thing?* The tank headed onto a trail that ran alongside a rocky slope. Thinking fast, Indy steered his horse up the slope to a parallel trail that carried him above the tank's position. When he was about twelve feet higher than the moving tank, Indy lifted both of his legs up, planted his boots on the saddle, and leaped from the horse.

Stretching out his arms and legs, Indy landed hard atop the trundling tank. He felt the wind get knocked out of him, but he refused to think of the pain. As the rapidly moving treads kicked up dust on either side, he thought only of his father, still trapped inside.

Indy pushed himself up from the back of the tank just as Vogel resurfaced through the hatch. Indy was about to reach for his bullwhip when he felt the wind knocked out of him again, this time because someone tackled him from the side.

The tank had veered away from the rocky wall, allowing a troop truck with five German soldiers in the back to draw up along the tank's left side. One of the soldiers had leaped from the troop carrier and knocked Indy down. The two men grappled as they rolled down the middle of the back of the tank and tried to avoid the treads whipping past them on either side. The soldier had drawn his

Luger, but Indy pinned his arm and belted him across the jaw.

Indy grabbed the gun from his opponent as two more soldiers leaped from the troop carrier to the tank. The first soldier, now deprived of his pistol, jumped up and was about to try and shove the American off the tank when Indy raised the Luger and fired. The bullet not only tore through the first soldier, but the two who had just moved directly behind him. As the three soldiers collapsed dead onto the back of the tank, Indy stared at the gun in disbelief.

But the fight wasn't over. A fourth soldier, wielding a combat knife, leaped from the truck and landed in front of Indy. Indy grabbed the soldier's wrist, but before Indy could raise the Luger, the soldier seized Indy's gun hand. Both men were struggling to keep their balance when Indy landed a punch across the man's jaw, then hurled himself against the man, knocking him back onto a cargo net behind the turret. The knife went flying out of the soldier's grip. Indy rolled away from the soldier and rose fast to stand beside the turret, and that's when Vogel made his move.

CHAPTER FOURTEEN

Vogel stepped out of the turret and picked up a metal chain that was rattling against the turret's side. While Indy's back was turned, Vogel clutched both ends of the chain as he threw it over Indy's head and pulled back hard. Indy felt the chain bite into his neck as he stumbled back into Vogel.

Indy and Vogel teetered atop the moving tank. As the soldier who had lost his knife began to get up from the cargo net where Indy had left him, Vogel twisted the chain and Indy suddenly found himself staring down into the turret's open hatch. Despite the chain that was choking him, Indy managed to shout, "Dad!"

Indy was still clutching the Luger in his right hand, and he was holding it in front of him when Vogel slammed him against the hatch. Indy's right wrist hit the hatch's metal rim and the Luger flew out of his hand and landed inside the tank.

"Dad!" Indy shouted again. "Dad! Get it!" He tensed his neck muscles as Vogel tugged him away from the hatch.

Inside the tank, Henry saw the Luger fall. But because a soldier inside the tank still had his own Luger aimed at Henry and Brody, all Henry could do was keep an eye on the fallen pistol and hope that none of the other soldiers noticed it.

As Vogel pulled Indy away from the hatch, Indy saw the other soldier — the one who had tried to stab him — step up and help Vogel. With the chain still around his neck and Vogel at his back, Indy swung out with his right arm and belted the soldier, knocking him onto the tank tread. The soldier screamed as the moving tread carried him forward and dropped him in front of the tank, which immediately rolled over him.

Indy threw all his weight backward against Vogel, who landed on the cargo net behind the turret. Inside the tank, Henry eyed the fallen Luger again and then glanced through a viewing port to see another troop truck speeding toward the tank. As he looked away from the port, the soldiers within the tank shifted positions. While one soldier kept his pistol aimed at Henry, the other went to a periscope, lowered its metal handgrips, and adjusted the scope to observe the action outside.

Outside the tank, the periscope rose up near Indy's

outstretched legs. Peering through the scope, the soldier saw Indy lying on top of Vogel but facing skyward, with the chain pulled taut across his throat. Indy lifted his feet and lunged forward toward the periscope, pulling Vogel with him.

Indy's face hit the lens of the periscope, causing the soldier who was watching him from below to flinch. Then the soldier — realizing what a great view he had — grinned and returned his eyes to the scope. A moment later, Vogel pulled back hard, yanking Indy back on top of him.

Down below, the soldier removed his hands from the periscope and turned to face his ally who was guarding Henry and Brody. The scope-operator laughed and said, "*Diese Amerikane. Sie Kampfen wie Weiber.*"

Up above, Indy's legs kicked out. His right boot smacked the periscope so hard that it spun. Below, the scope's metal handgrips spun as well, and whacked the scope-operator in the back of the head so hard that he collapsed against the other soldier, who stumbled back.

The periscope-struck soldier landed on Henry, but Henry shoved him aside and accidentally onto Marcus, and then Henry moved fast for the fallen Luger. But no sooner had Henry wrapped his left hand around the gun than the other soldier jumped at Henry and grabbed his wrist. The soldier maneuvered himself behind Henry, who managed to twist the gun's muzzle back toward his attacker before he realized that he was more likely to shoot his own head off if he pulled the trigger.

While Henry struggled with the soldier, Vogel rolled Indy off him and tried to push Indy's head down onto the treads. Indy felt the treads brush against the side of his face. Vogel was stronger than he looked. Vogel pressed harder and the treads scraped flesh from Indy's left cheek.

Within the tank, the soldier was still behind Henry when he managed to get hold of Henry's Luger. With his left hand, Henry grabbed the soldier's wrist and tried to angle the gun's muzzle away from his body. As Henry felt his grip begin to slip, he reached into his vest pocket with his right hand and removed his fountain pen. Henry lifted the pen and squirted ink back over his left shoulder and directly into the soldier's eyes.

The soldier grimaced and squeezed his eyes shut, and Henry pushed himself back against the man, slamming his wrist into a metal bar and his head against the wall of the tank. The Luger instantly fell from his hand and clattered on the floor.

As the soldier collapsed behind Henry, Brody scrambled up from under the other soldier and said, "Henry, the pen . . ."

"What?" Henry said with a startled expression.

"But don't you see?" Brody said with a delighted grin. "The pen is mightier than the sword!"

Henry jumped up from the floor. The tank's driver was staring out the front viewing port, unaware that Henry and Brody were no longer under guard. Henry glanced out a port to see that the troop truck he'd glimpsed earlier was now drawing even with the tank's right side. Henry moved behind the tank's right side cannon, slipped his finger around the trigger, and fired at almost point-blank range straight at the troop truck.

The truck was knocked off its wheels as it exploded, launching soldiers high into the air. The power of the blast threw Vogel off of Indy, sending both men onto the tank's left tread, with Indy in the lead on a trip to the font of the tank. To avoid being dragged under the treads, Indy rolled his body hard over the side. He grabbed onto the shredded cannon — the one he had jammed the stone into — that protruded from the tank's side.

With his left cheek hurting like blazes from the gashes made by tank tread, Indy clung to the damaged cannon. The tank was traveling parallel to a wall of rock at Indy's left, so close that the cannon's erupted muzzle nearly brushed against it. Indy hoped that Vogel had failed to roll off of the tread, but a moment later, he glanced up to see Vogel standing atop the tank once again. Evidently, Vogel had rolled in the other direction.

Indy reached up to the edge of the tank to pull himself back up. Vogel moved closer to the edge and stomped on Indy's fingers. Indy wrapped both arms around the cannon and hung on for dear life.

Vogel could have drawn his pistol and shot Indy, but that would have given him little satisfaction. From the tank's cargo net, Vogel removed a long-handled metal shovel. He returned to the edge of the tank and brought the shovel down on Indy's hands. Indy groaned in pain, but held tight to the cannon.

Within the tank, Henry returned his pen to his vest pocket as he stepped away from the right side cannon. Brody gazed from the cannon to Henry in astonishment and said, "Look what you did!"

"It's war!" Henry said, without pleasure. Motioning Brody to the steps that led out of the hatch, he added, "Didn't I tell you it was a rescue, huh?" But just as Henry began climbing up after Brody, he felt powerful arms grab at the back of his jacket and yank him back down into the tank. He was under attack by the soldier that he thought had been knocked unconscious — the one whose face was stained by the ink from Henry's pen.

While Henry resumed his fight with the soldier, Vogel brought the shovel down on Indy's fingers yet again. Indy grimaced, his injured hands losing their grip. But instead of falling to the rocky ground, he stopped short. His bag's shoulder strap had become tangled around the end of the damaged side cannon. His legs dragged below him, kicking up dirt and dust — but he was alive.

The tank veered closer to the parallel wall, and the cannon's broken end began dragging against the rock, spilling dirt and stones down on top of Indy. He gasped and tried to wriggle free of his shoulder strap, but could not. Desperate to escape, he began tugging on the strap, trying to break it, but the only effect was that he felt the strap jerk sharply under his right arm. Dangling beside the tank, he turned to look up ahead and saw that the wall beside the tank ended at a rocky outcrop, which jutted out from the wall at almost a right angle.

Vogel saw the outcrop too. He moved over to crouch beside the turret and shouted a command to the driver. In response, the driver laughed and steered even closer to the rocky wall on the left, narrowing the gap between Indy and the wall.

Indy realized the driver was trying to crush him and he twisted his body sideways. He howled as heavier stones began raining down. His eyes went wide with fear as he watched the outcrop coming up fast. He had no reason to doubt that his death was only seconds away.

While the tank's driver focused on his target, he remained unaware of the battle raging only a few feet behind him. The ink-stained soldier wrestled Henry to the floor, and then both men saw the Luger that Henry had knocked from the soldier's hand earlier — the same weapon that Indy had dropped through the hatch.

The soldier reached for the Luger first. He was about to pull the trigger when he saw something stir in the corner of his vision. Turning his head, he saw Brody kneeling on the steps below the open hatch, holding a cylindrical artillery shell. Before the soldier could react, Brody brought it down hard over his head.

Still clutching the Luger, the stunned soldier fell backwards, and as he fell, he discharged the gun at the tank's ceiling. Sparks flew as the bullet ricocheted several times through the tank's interior, until it finally pinged off the metal above the front port and slammed into the driver's head. Blood flowed from under the driver's hat, and his body slumped forward.

As the dead driver's body depressed the steering levers, the tank veered sharply to the right. Vogel was unprepared for the sudden turn that sent the tank away from the rocky outcrop, and he was thrown down in front of the turret, onto an expanse of metal just below the main cannon.

Indy felt a brief but incredible sense of relief as the tank veered away from the outcrop — but the relief was quickly replaced by overwhelming rage. He grunted as he pulled himself up onto the cannon, worked his bag's strap free from the barrel, and hauled himself back onto the tank. Vogel was just rising from the area in front of the turret when Indy seized him by his jacket and launched his fist right into Vogel's face. Vogel fell backward and vanished over the side.

Leaning over the turret's hatch, Indy shouted, "Dad?"

Henry popped his head up through the hatch. He laughed and said sarcastically, "You call this archaeology?"

"Get out of there, Dad!" Indy said, tugging his father up through the hatch. And then they helped Brody out, so that all three men were standing on the back of the tank. That was when Vogel rematerialized.

Vogel had not fallen off the tank, only down in front of the turret again. After recovering himself, he grabbed the long-handled shovel and scrambled over the turret. Indy saw Vogel coming and barely dodged the Nazi's vicious swing. The shovel made a whooshing sound as it whipped past Indy's stomach.

Vogel swung at Indy's head, but Indy ducked and caught the shovel with his left hand. Behind Indy, Brody said, "How does one get off this thing?"

Brody got his answer when Indy wound back his right arm and his elbow knocked Brody off the back of the tank and onto the ground. Then Indy sent his fist into Vogel's jaw. Vogel stumbled back and fell over the turret's hatch. His hat fell off his head and landed somewhere within the tank.

Henry had not seen Brody's departure. He turned to Indy, looked around, and said, "Where's Marcus?"

Before Indy could reply, Vogel pushed himself away from the turret and swung the shovel at Indy. Indy ducked. The shovel hit Henry, and Henry fell over onto the left tread. Henry howled as his body bounced along the tread, heading for the front of the tank.

Moving with lightning speed, Indy reached for his bullwhip at his side, backhanded Vogel, then lashed out with his whip. The end of the whip wrapped around Henry's right ankle, and Henry yelped again.

Holding tight to the whip with both hands while his father bounced on the tread like a rag doll, Indy shouted, "Hang on, Dad!"

Henry yelled again. And then, while Indy struggled to save his father, Vogel came up behind Indy and punched him in the back. Indy gritted his teeth, but refused to let go of the whip.

Suddenly, a mounted figure came riding up fast behind the tank. It was Sallah on the horse he had taken from Donovan's caravan. As Sallah drew up along the left side of the tank, he tipped his fez to Henry and shouted, "Father of Indy, give me your hand!"

Vogel slid one arm around Indy's neck and struck him again in the back with the other. Indy shouted, "Sallah! Get Dad!"

"Give me your hand!" Sallah shouted again. As Henry reached out and Sallah grabbed hold of him, Indy flung his whip aside. Years of excavation work had made Sallah extremely strong, and he had no difficulty holding Henry aloft until his horse carried them away from the tank.

Vogel tried to choke Indy, but now that he had both hands free, Indy didn't hesitate to use them. He drove his elbow into Vogel's stomach and twisted Vogel's left arm up behind his back. Then Indy turned Vogel to face the back of the turret and slammed his head into it. Then he did it again. And again.

Indy was still unleashing his rage when he felt a strange shift in the air pressure. He lifted his gaze and looked ahead, only to see that the land appeared to fall away in front of them. The tank was heading straight for the edge of a high cliff.

Indy saw that Sallah had stopped his horse near the cliff's edge, and that his father was all right. And then a strong wind blew Indy's hat right off his head, and his face filled with horror as he realized he might have missed his last chance to jump off the tank.

Leaving Vogel draped over the turret, Indy's arms flailed as he threw himself backwards and rolled down the back of the tank, just as the front began to dip over the edge. The tank trundled over the cliff and plummeted.

Vogel clung tight to the turret and screamed his head off until the tank met the rocks far, far below.

Brody had just caught up with Henry and Sallah when they saw the tank vanish at the edge of the high plateau, and then they heard the crash. Sallah climbed down from his horse, and then all three men were running to the cliff's edge. Henry got there first.

"Junior?!" Henry shouted.

The tank exploded.

"Indy!" Sallah cried.

Smoke billowed from the tank as it continued to roll down the base of the cliff.

Henry scanned the ground below, searching for any sign of his son, but then his face fell with a sudden realization. "Oh, God," he gasped. "I've lost him." Henry's lower lip trembled. "And I never told him anything." He tried to look at Brody, but couldn't tear his gaze from the burning tank. "I just wasn't ready, Marcus. Five minutes would have been enough."

Just a short distance away, a tangle of dried-out roots shifted in the dirt at the cliff's edge. Hatless and battered, but otherwise breathing, Indiana Jones pulled himself up and over onto relatively firm ground. Rising to his feet, he turned to see his father and two friends standing dangerously close to the edge of the cliff, gazing down at something. Dazed and bewildered, he staggered up behind them, came to a stop beside his father, and followed their gaze to the wrecked tank far below. Nodding his head at the wreck, Indy gasped and caught his breath.

It took a moment for Henry to realize that it wasn't Sallah or Brody who had moved up beside him. Henry turned, saw Indy, and his mouth fell open. And then he threw his arms around his son and murmured, "I thought I'd lost you, boy!"

Indy's head began to clear, and he became aware of his father's embrace. Indy couldn't remember the last time his father had ever held him like that, if ever. But it touched him and he put his arms around his father, patted his back, and replied, "I thought you had too, sir."

Sallah and Brody watched silently as Henry and Indy embraced. Sallah knew it was a very special moment, and not just because Indy had survived. While Sallah beamed with happy appreciation and felt proud to be a witness to Indy's reconciliation with Henry, Brody looked from Indy to the tank and then back to Indy again, trying to sort out how Indy could be standing in front of them at all.

Pulling away from Indy and regaining mastery of his emotions, Henry said, "Well . . ." He clapped Indy's upper arms and finished, "Well done. Come on." Henry stepped away from the exhausted Indy, who promptly collapsed in a barely upright position.

Brody and Sallah followed Henry away from the edge

of the cliff and back to Sallah's horse. As Henry walked, he added, "Let's go, then." But then he stopped, turned to see that Indy wasn't walking with them, and he shouted back, "Why are you sitting there resting when we're so near the end?! Come on, let's go!"

Indy thought he would just sit there a while longer, but then a sudden gust of wind delivered his fedora from out of nowhere. As his hat rolled to a stop in front of his knees, Indy thought, *Maybe it* is *time to get moving.*

Chapter FIFTEEN

Walter Donovan and Elsa Schneider stood beside their open car, which was parked atop a high plateau overlooking a wide desert. Shortly after Colonel Vogel had taken the tank to pursue Indiana Jones, Donovan and Elsa had driven off in another direction along with the remains of their caravan and did their best to follow the map from Henry Jones' diary. While the German and Turkish soldiers kept watch nearby, Donovan peered through binoculars to view the upper rim of a narrow canyon; from his perspective, it looked like a C-shaped gorge that curved across the desert floor.

Lowering the binoculars, Donovan wore an astonished expression as he continued gazing at the gorge and said, "The Canyon of the Crescent Moon."

Elsa took the binoculars and peered through them. Indeed, it appeared that Donovan had found the legendary canyon. And if the ancient text on the Grail tablet was correct, the canyon would lead them to the temple where they would find the Holy Grail itself.

Sallah had rounded up the horses that Indy had been forced to release earlier, including the horse that had carried Indy to the tank. Hoping to recover the camels later, Sallah joined Indy, Henry, and Brody as they continued on horseback, making their way to the Canyon of the Crescent Moon.

Indy reached to the upper left side of his cheek and felt the wounds he had gained from the tank tread. He'd stopped bleeding and the pain wasn't too bad. He never wanted to add more scars to his collection, but the way he figured things, a few more scars were nothing compared to outright death.

Although Henry had never been to the Canyon of the Crescent Moon, he remembered the details of his map well enough to lead the way. Soon, the four men found Donovan's car and other vehicles abandoned at the mouth of a gorge that traveled through mountainous sandstone rocks, too narrow for the vehicles to enter. Henry and Indy went first, maneuvering their horses slowly along the shadowy floor of the gorge. Sallah and Brody followed.

Eventually, the gorge delivered them to an open area that faced a towering wall of rock illuminated by a broad shaft of sunlight. Carved directly into the sandstone cliff was a spectacular architectural façade, the remains of a hidden city, which displayed obvious Grecian influence. The men gaped at the sight of the colossal columns that lined the façade's entrance. Indy guessed the entire structure was around 150 feet tall.

The men dismounted, leaving their horses behind as they walked toward the structure. They climbed a flight of wide stone steps to arrive before a dark, rectangular doorway. Indy had reloaded his revolver, and Sallah also carried a pistol. Indy got his gun out and entered the doorway first. The other men followed silently.

They crept through a twisting, shadowy passage with rough-hewn walls until they heard a voice up ahead, someone speaking in German. They paused for a moment and then moved forward to peek around a corner that offered a view into a large chamber. It was a temple, with a broad stone floor embedded with a metal seal, and reliefs carved into the high walls. Standing in the temple was Donovan with about a dozen Turkish soldiers and just a few Nazis, all of whom were looking away from Indy's group, facing a stairway that led up into another passage. The stairway was bracketed by stone statues of knights and a pair of monstrous lions.

Indy, Henry, Sallah, and Brody lowered themselves behind some rocks that offered some protective cover as they watched Donovan's men. From what Indy could see, the men were all focused on one Turkish soldier in particular; the Turk held his sword out in front of him and had just begun moving cautiously up the steps to the next passage. At the bottom of the steps, a Nazi soldier held a pistol out, but Indy couldn't tell whether the pistol was aimed at the passage's entrance or the ascending Turk's back.

The Turkish soldier was nervous and sweating hard as he walked slowly into the passage. The passage's walls were dark and lined with thick cobwebs. When he glanced down at the floor, he saw one of his fellow soldiers lying on the ground; the soldier's eyes were closed and his mouth agape. Because the passage was so dark, it took a moment for the walking Turk to realize that the fallen soldier's head was lying *beside* his body, which had been neatly decapitated.

The walking Turk gasped, but held tight to his sword and stepped forward. He knew that if he turned back, the Nazi soldier would shoot him. His eyes were wide with terror when he heard what sounded like a distant beast's roar, and then the roar became louder. A sudden rush of air traveled toward him, making the cobwebs shiver, and then there was a whooshing sound. The last thing that the soldier heard was a clang as something struck his sword's blade.

Even from his hiding place, Indy had felt the surge of air that blew out from the upper passage, but he could only imagine what had happened to the Turkish soldier. A moment later, Indy had his answer when the Turk's head tumbled out of the passage and rolled past Donovan and the other soldiers. It was then, as a white-shirted figure near Donovan turned with a horrified expression, that Indy saw Elsa's face. The Turk's head didn't stop rolling until it thudded against the base of the rock that concealed Indy. Indy kept his own head low.

Donovan turned to the pistol-wielding Nazi soldier and said, "Helmut, another volunteer."

Helmut and a fellow Nazi grabbed another Turk and shoved him toward the passage's entrance. As the Turk protested and struggled, Brody cringed and looked away from the sight, only to face a group of Nazi soldiers who had snuck up behind him. The soldiers surged forward, leveling their guns at Indy and each member of his party.

Indy raised his hands. The Nazis took his gun and Sallah's pistol.

Donovan heard the commotion from behind, and signaled the Nazi soldiers to release the "volunteer." The other Nazis escorted Indy, Henry, Sallah, and Brody to stand before Donovan.

Elsa stepped past Donovan to face Indy. "I never expected to see you again."

"I'm like a bad penny," Indy said with a sneer. "I always turn up."

"Step back now, Dr. Schneider," Donovan said. "Give Dr. Jones some room. He's going to recover the Grail for us."

Indy laughed in Donovan's face.

"Impossible?" Donovan said, eyeing Indy cagily. "What do you say, Jones? Ready to go down in history?"

"As what?" Indy said. "A Nazi stooge, like you?"

Wincing with distaste, Donovan answered him scornfully. "Nazis?! Is that the limit of your vision? The Nazis want to write themselves into the Grail legend . . . take on the world. Well, they're welcome. But I want the Grail itself."

Indy and his father were standing beside each other, and they exchanged glances to confirm they were both thinking the same thing: Donovan was a lunatic.

"The cup that gives everlasting life," Donovan continued. "Hitler can have the world, but he can't take it with him. I'm going to be drinking my own health when he's gone the way of the dodo."

Donovan drew a small pistol from his pocket and aimed it at Indy as he backed away slowly, putting some distance between them. "The Grail is mine," Donovan said, "and you're going to get it for me."

Staring hard into Donovan's eyes, Indy said, "Shooting me won't get you anywhere."

"You know something, Dr. Jones? You're absolutely right." Donovan shifted his aim just slightly, pulled the trigger, and shot Henry. The bullet entered Henry's side, just below the ribs. Henry gasped and clutched at his side as his body pivoted to face his son.

"Dad?" Indy said, gripping his father's shoulders. "Dad?!"

"Junior . . ." Henry rasped out, and then fell forward against Indy.

"No!" Elsa shouted with concern as she moved toward Indy and Henry.

"Get back!" Donovan shouted to Elsa as she stepped in front of him. Elsa stopped in her tracks.

Brody and Sallah rushed over to help Indy lower Henry to the floor. Blood was flowing from the wound. Indy unbuttoned and pushed back his father's shirt, then grabbed a handkerchief from Sallah and pressed it against the wound to stanch the flow.

And then the rage overcame Indy. With murder in his eyes, he rose fast and spun toward Donovan, but saw that Donovan once again had the gun leveled at him.

"You can't save him when you're dead," Donovan said. "The healing power of the Grail is the only thing that can save your father now. It's time to ask yourself what you believe."

Indy had seen some incredible things in his lifetime, but he still wasn't convinced that the Grail existed, let alone that it possessed the power to save his father. However, there was one thing he believed with utmost certainty: If he didn't at least try to go after the Grail, Donovan would probably shoot Sallah and Brody, too — or try to send them into the passage.

Indy couldn't let that happen.

All the soldiers who surrounded Indy and his allies now stepped back, leaving a clear path between Indy and the steps that led past the monstrous lion statues to the upper passage. Indy carried his father's Grail diary as he walked slowly toward the passage's entrance. He also carried his whip, which dangled at his side. At least the Nazis had left him with that.

As he climbed the steps, he opened the diary to the pages his father had shown him when they had been on the zeppelin. In a low whisper, he read aloud, "'The Breath of God . . . only the penitent man will pass.'"

He lifted his gaze from the diary as he continued up the steps. Struggling to find the meaning of the words, he repeated, "'The penitent man will pass.'"

At the top of the steps, Indy stopped and glanced back into the chamber. He looked at his father, saw that he was still breathing, and then turned to proceed into the passage.

"The penitent man will pass," Indy whispered again to himself. "The penitent man . . ." He looked down and saw the bodies of the two decapitated Turks who had preceded him.

In the temple chamber behind Indy, Henry lay on the floor, looking up at the ceiling as he contemplated the words he remembered from his diary. Unintentionally echoing his son, Henry rasped, "'Only the penitent man will pass. Only the penitent man will pass.'"

In the passage, Indy's eyes flicked to the passage's cobweb-covered walls. "The penitent man will pass," he repeated again. Holding the diary out in front of him to push the cobwebs aside, he muttered, "The penitent, penitent . . . The penitent man . . ." His eyes and ears were alert for the slightest movement, and he repeated the words without thinking about them, as if they might be a mantra that would lead him to enlightenment, or at least allow him to keep his head affixed to his neck. And out of this rhythm of words evolved a slight variation, as Indy said aloud, "The penitent man is humble before God. Penitent man is humble . . ."

Then the passage seemed to breathe, and Indy saw the cobwebs begin to move.

". . . kneels before God."

As Indy was hit by a rush of wind, he shouted, "Kneel!"

Obeying his own command, Indy dropped to his knees and instinctively rolled forward. There was an immediate grinding sound from overhead and behind him. When he came to a stop, he sat up beside an ancient gear mechanism made of wooden wheels. Somehow, he had activated the wheels, which were still moving. A length of rope dangled from the wall, and he looped it around one of the spinning wheels, jamming the mechanism.

Indy looked back to see a pair of large, rotating discs of metal with razor-sharp edges: one traveled out at an angle from a concealed slot in the wall, and the other pushed up through a similar slot in the floor. Because he had jammed the wooden mechanism, both circular blades stopped turning.

Catching his breath, Indy shouted back through the passage, "I'm through!"

In the outer chamber, Donovan and Elsa heard Indy's cry. Donovan said, "We're through."

Brody and Sallah heard, too, and they smiled with relief. Sallah was holding Henry, and looked down at him and said, "He's all right."

But Henry shook his head and said, "No."

Unaware of his father's negative response, Indy stood a short distance from the disabled blades as he consulted the diary again. "The second challenge: 'The Word of God. Only in the footsteps of God will he proceed.'" Brushing a layer of sticky cobwebs off the brim of his hat, he turned slowly and began to proceed deeper into the passage.

"The Word of God . . ." Indy repeated. "The Word of . . ."

He arrived before a thick curtain of cobwebs. Pulling them aside with his hand, he looked down to see that the passage floor extended with a cobblestone path. Each cobble was engraved with a letter. Turning the words of the second challenge over in his mind, Indy said, "Proceed in the footsteps of the Word."

While Indy examined the cobblestones, Brody and Sallah watched as Henry lifted his head painfully and said, "'The Word of God . . .'"

Thinking Henry was delirious, Brody said, "No, Henry. Try not to talk."

Henry lowered his head, which Sallah cradled carefully with his hands. Looking again at the chamber's ceiling, Henry rasped, "The name of God."

The words came to Indy at the same time. "The name of God . . ." he said, his gaze sweeping over the cobblestones. "Jehovah."

Unfortunately, Indy could not hear his father's coincidental caution, which Henry muttered out: "But in the Latin alphabet, 'Jehovah' begins with an 'I.'"

Hovering beside Henry, Sallah and Brody looked at each other with concern. They were both now convinced that Henry was just rambling.

In the passage, Indy said aloud, "J," and took a step forward onto a cobblestone that bore that letter. Immediately, the stone broke away and Indy crashed down through a hole in the floor. His arms shot out and he clutched the edges of the hole. For a moment, his legs dangled over a deep pit, but he grunted and pulled himself up through the hole. Incredibly, he had managed to hang onto the Grail diary.

"Idiot!" Indy cursed himself, and then muttered, "In Latin, 'Jehovah' starts with an 'I.'" He found the cobblestone that he was looking for and said aloud as he stepped onto it, "I." Then he moved to a stone at his left and said, "E." He moved to "H" without difficulty, but when he landed on "O," he found himself saying, "Oh!" as the stone behind him pivoted slightly, nearly knocking him off balance. He proceeded. "V . . . A."

With some relief at having passed the second challenge, Indy arrived before a passage that was so narrow that he had to move sideways to walk its length. As he moved through it, he saw the silhouette of a carved lion's head that jutted out from one of the walls above him.

The passage ended at a sheer drop into a chasm that receded into darkness and which faced another wall of rock that appeared to be about a hundred feet away. Indy wouldn't even try to guess the chasm's depth. It looked bottomless, and he couldn't see any way to reach the opposite wall.

"'The Path of God,'" he said aloud. Strangely, there was something familiar about the chasm. He peered back into the passage, looked up at the lion's head, and then he remembered the medieval painting he'd seen in his father's home, the one that depicted a knight walking on thin air between two cliffs. He also recalled that his father had done a pen-and-ink sketch of that painting in his diary. Indy thumbed through the diary until he found the sketch, and he recited from memory, "'Only in the leap from the lion's head will he prove his worth.'"

Indy looked down and around his position again. "Impossible," he said. "Nobody can jump this."

Just then, he heard a distant cry of pain echo up from the passage behind him. A moment later, Brody's voice called out, "Indy! Indy, you must hurry! Come quickly!"

Indy knew his father was dying, and he wanted to run back through the passage and return to his father's side, but then he thought, *What if the Grail really can save Dad?*

And that's when it all hit him. Gazing forward at the empty air that stretched out between him and the far wall, he said, "It's a leap of faith." But then he glanced down again and said, "Oh, geez . . ."

While Indy tried to think around and through his situation, Henry gasped out from the temple chamber, "You must believe, boy. You must . . . believe."

Indy put his hand over his heart, took a few deep breaths, and closed his eyes. When he opened his eyes again, he felt almost relaxed with the idea of what he was about to do. And then he did it: He lifted his left foot and fell forward.

CHAPTER SIXTEEN

*I*ndy's arms went out at his sides, as if he might catch himself somehow before he plummeted to the rocks below, but then his left foot landed on something hard. It felt like a stone floor — an invisible stone floor — and then his right foot landed beside his left. Astonished, and wondering what exactly he was standing on, Indy held still for a moment, but then he shifted his head slightly to realize he was standing on a painted pathway. And then he figured out how.

Ingeniously, the first Crusaders had painted the surface of a stone bridge to create an illusion that aligned the bridge with the rocks below. The illusion only worked if one were standing below the lion's head at the end of the passage, and as Indy moved forward, the forced-perspective painting on the bridge became more obvious. Because the bridge was only about three feet wide and without railings, he moved very carefully.

After Indy crossed the "invisible" bridge, he saw some loose sand lying at the edge of the far wall. He bent down, scooped up a handful of sand, and then turned and tossed it out across the bridge. The scattered sand revealed the bridge's surface area, which would allow him to return safely.

The passage at the other end was so small that he had to crawl through it. He got down on his hands and knees and moved through until he emerged within a chamber illuminated by numerous torches. The torches cast a golden glow throughout the chamber, which had an altar displaying a vast array of chalices. The chalices were in different shapes and sizes, from small metal cups to large goblets, and most appeared to be made of gold or silver. There were possibly more than a hundred chalices in all.

But to Indy, the most amazing thing in the chamber was the knight.

The knight knelt before the altar, his back to Indy. He wore a cowl and gloves that were made of chain mail, and a gray cape covered his back. An ancient book was spread open on a stone bench in front of him, and his head was lowered over it. A shining sword rested against the edge of the bench beside his right hand, and he didn't move as Indy stepped up behind him. For a moment, Indy wondered if the knight's armor housed a skeleton or if it were merely empty.

But then the knight slowly raised his head.

Indy was speechless. Remembering his father's condition, he glanced at the chalices and wondered, *Why are there so many?*

Without warning, the knight reached for the sword as he stood up, and then swung the blade at Indy. Indy easily dodged the sword, which the knight then raised high over his head as he prepared to strike again. The knight's face was visible then, and Indy saw that he was a very old man with a white beard and mustache.

But the knight's attack ended there. Holding the sword overhead, he gasped at his effort, and then the sword's weight carried him backwards so that he fell on top of the stone bench behind him, right beside the book he had been reading.

"Oh," moaned the knight as Indy stepped over to help him up to a sitting position on the bench. The knight looked up at Indy and then smiled. In a deep voice, he said, "I knew you'd come . . ." Then the knight shook his head and finished, ". . . but my strength has left me."

Seeing the knight up close, Indy saw that his flesh, like his armor and cape, was gray, as if all color had been drained from him. Indy said, "Who are you?"

"The last of the three brothers who swore an oath to find the Grail and to guard it."

Indy's mind reeled. He said, "That was seven hundred years ago."

"A long time to wait," the knight said with a solemn nod. Still seated, he reached up to touch Indy's hat and said, "You're strangely dressed . . . for a knight."

As the knight examined Indy's bullwhip, Indy said, "I'm not exactly . . ." Catching himself, Indy said, "A knight? What do you mean?"

"I was chosen because I was the bravest, the most worthy. The honor was mine until another came to challenge me to single combat." Lifting his sword and holding it out to Indy, the knight said, "I pass it to you who vanquished me."

Indy gulped, then shook his head slightly. "Listen," he said, "I don't have time to explain, but —"

Indy was interrupted by a shuffling sound from behind. He turned, and then both he and the knight directed their gazes to the chamber's small opening. Donovan, clutching his gun in his right hand, came through first. He was followed by Elsa.

Indy stayed close to the knight. Both Donovan and Elsa gave the knight a cursory glance before their eyes fell upon the display of chalices. Dumbstruck by the sight, they moved forward toward the altar, searching for the Holy Grail amongst the gleaming cups and goblets that reflected the dancing light of the surrounding torches.

After gazing at the chalices for several seconds, Donovan turned with a perplexed expression to look directly at the knight and ask, "Which one is it?"

"You must choose," the knight replied. A moment later, he added, "But choose wisely. For as the true Grail will bring you life, the false Grail will take it from you."

"I'm not a historian," Donovan said as he surveyed the chalices. "I have no idea what it looks like. Which one is it?"

Moving behind Donovan, Elsa said, "Let me choose."

"Thank you, Doctor," Donovan said. Elsa smiled at him, and then she turned her attention to the chalices.

The knight looked to Indy, and Indy returned his gaze. Both were curious about whether Elsa would find the Grail, but Indy was more curious about what would happen if she didn't.

Elsa reached out with her black-gloved hands to pick up a solid gold goblet encrusted with emeralds. Still smiling, she handed it to Donovan, who took it and sighed, "Oh, yes." Holding the goblet out before him, he marveled at it and remarked, "It's more beautiful than I'd ever imagined!"

Elsa continued to smile, but then she glanced at Indy and her smile melted away. Indy caught something in her gaze, a certain look that told him that maybe, just maybe, she really had learned something from her mistakes, and that she had just done something to try and make amends — or was it to further her own ends?

A large basin of water was on a table across from the altar. As Donovan carried the goblet to the basin, he said, "This certainly is the cup of the King of Kings." He dipped the goblet into the basin, filled it with water, raised it as if making a toast, and said, "Eternal life." And then he raised the goblet to his lips, closed his eyes, and drank the water.

Donovan's eyes were still closed as he slowly lowered the goblet from his face. He sighed with satisfaction at his accomplishment, but a moment later, his eyes opened and he gasped again as he bent forward over the water-filled basin in a painful convulsion. Staring into the basin, he saw his face reflected in the water and saw that his skin appeared to be sagging below his eyes.

Donovan turned away from the basin and looked at the backs of his hands, where liver spots and wrinkles had suddenly formed. Trembling, he raised his gaze to Elsa and rasped, "What ... is happening ... to me?" He lurched forward and grabbed Elsa by her shoulders.

Elsa gasped and screamed as Donovan began to age rapidly in front of her. A moment after he gripped her shoulders, his silver hair suddenly sprouted, growing long, gray, and brittle. Donovan shouted, "Tell me, what ... is ... happening?!"

Indy froze, horrified by the sight of Donovan's transformation. Beside him, the seated knight barely stirred.

Elsa shrieked as Donovan's skin turned brown and leathery, stretching across his bones until it cracked and split. His eyeballs shrank back into his skull as he raised his boney hands to Elsa's throat and tried to choke her.

Indy rushed forward and pulled Elsa toward him as he pushed Donovan's fury-driven remains away. Donovan's skeleton fell back against the wall and shattered, exploding into dust. Elsa clung to Indy and kept right on screaming.

Indy stared at the heap of bones and dust on the floor. A sudden wind whipped through the chamber and blew back the dust beside what was left of Donovan's skull. The dust shifted to reveal a small metal pin with a black swastika in the middle of it. Evidently, Donovan — for all his claims otherwise — had been a member of the Nazi party after all.

The knight looked to Indy and Elsa and said, "He chose . . . poorly."

Indy held the knight's gaze for a moment, but then he moved to the altar and looked at all the ornate chalices. Elsa followed him and said, "It would not be made out of gold."

Indy's eyes came to rest on a simple earthenware cup

that sat behind some metal chalices that appeared to be far more valuable. "That's the cup of a carpenter." Elsa looked at it doubtfully, but Indy was determined, and said, "There's only one way to find out."

Indy glanced at the knight as he walked over to the water basin. He filled the cup, but paused for a moment as he remembered what had become of Donovan. But then Indy thought of his father, and it was with that thought that he raised the cup to his lips and took several large swallows.

Indy turned fast and looked at the knight. As he turned, Indy felt a strange sensation at his upper left cheek. Reaching up to the side of his face, he touched the place where the tank tread had cut into his flesh. But instead of touching wounds, he felt smooth skin above the whiskers along his jaw. Indy's wounds had been healed.

The knight said, "You have chosen wisely. But the Grail cannot pass beyond the Great Seal. That is the boundary and the price of immortality."

Indy remembered the metal seal as he refilled the Grail, and Elsa followed him as he left the knight behind and carried the Grail back to the chamber where he'd left his father. Brody and Sallah were still with Henry, trying to comfort him, but his flesh had assumed a deathly pallor from all the blood he'd lost. The soldiers stepped aside as Indy returned. Henry's eyes were closed, and he had been about to breathe his last when Indy lowered the Grail to his lips.

Henry drank from the Grail, but some of the water ran down the corners of his mouth. Sallah tilted Henry's head forward so the water would flow more easily. After Henry had gulped some down, Indy moved the Grail over the wound on his father's side and poured the remaining water directly onto it. Henry winced and steam rose from his flesh, but then, to everyone's astonishment, the blood washed away and the wound disappeared.

Looking to his father's face, Indy saw the pallor had left and his color had returned. Henry's eyes opened, and he gazed up at the ceiling for a moment as if he were trying to remember where he was. Then, he noticed Indy. Seeing his son, Henry beamed. And then Henry saw the cup in his son's hands.

Henry reached up and touched the Grail. He looked at Indy with questioning eyes, and from Indy's smile he knew the answer. *Yes, it's the Holy Grail, Dad.*

Henry took the Grail and held it. It felt so much lighter than he'd imagined, and he could barely believe that he was actually holding the object that he had spent most of his life searching for.

Elsa stood just a short distance away, staring at the Grail with wonder. The Turkish soldiers were awestruck by the sight of the Grail and Henry's recovery, and they threw down their weapons and fled from the temple. Sallah snatched up a fallen rifle and leveled it at the Nazis. "Drop your weapons," Sallah said. "Please."

The remaining soldiers dropped their weapons and raised their hands in surrender.

Indy was still kneeling beside his father. "Dad, come on. Get to your feet." As he helped his father up, Henry left the Grail on the floor.

Elsa bent down and picked up the Grail. Indy noticed Elsa's action, and then Henry saw her, too. She took a few steps across the chamber, and then turned to Indy and said, "We have got it! Come on!" She started to back up, moving across the metal seal in the floor toward the passage that led back outside.

"Elsa!" Indy said and took a cautious step forward. "Elsa, don't move!"

"It's ours, Indy," Elsa said, holding the Grail out in front of her. "Yours and mine." She took another couple of step backwards, and there came a rumbling sound from all around the temple as she arrived at the seal's center.

"Elsa, don't cross the seal," Indy said firmly. "The knight warned us not to take the Grail from here."

The rumbling continued, and Elsa looked around nervously. Indy looked toward the chamber walls, and then dust and dirt suddenly rained down from the ceiling. The floor began quaking, and Elsa was knocked off balance. As she fell upon the seal, the Grail bounced away from her grasp and rolled across the floor. A crack opened up in the stone floor directly below the Grail, and then the crack became a split. Elsa scrambled up from the floor and lunged for the Grail.

Elsa landed on top of the split, but the broken floor to her left rose suddenly, and the split widened, throwing her off balance again. The tips of her gloved fingers bumped into the Grail, knocking it into the crevasse. The Grail landed on a small, rocky ledge below, and Elsa found herself slipping off the edge of the broken, rising floor.

The temple was in chaos. Sallah and Brody felt the floor beneath them tilt back at a steep angle. The remaining soldiers leaped across the chasm and dodged falling rocks in a desperate effort to escape. Henry stumbled, and Indy grabbed him and picked him up.

Elsa clung to the upper edge of the widening crevasse and screamed. She lost her grip, slipped down to a shallow ledge, and kicked off, hurling herself across the gap to land on her stomach on the opposite floor. But that floor began to tip up, too, and Elsa's legs kicked at empty air as she began to slide off the edge.

Seeing Elsa's position, Indy dived away from his father's side and slid headfirst down the inclined stone floor, skidding across the small, loose stones that now shifted and bounced across the upended floor's surface. Spreading his legs out behind him, he launched his arms forward and caught Elsa's hands in his just as she fell away from the floor.

Elsa's eyes were wide with fear as she clutched at Indy's wrists and her body swung out over the dark abyss. Above and behind Indy, Henry shouted, "Junior! Junior!"

Elsa turned her head to see the Grail resting on the nearby ledge. Indy knew what she was thinking. Muscles straining, he gasped, "Elsa —"

Too late. She jerked her left hand free of his grip and extended her arm out, reaching for the Grail. Indy's suddenly empty right hand flew beside his left to clamp onto Elsa's right gloved hand.

Elsa swayed slightly as she tried to grab the Grail. It was only a few inches beyond her grasp. Above her, Indy said, "Elsa, don't. Elsa ..."

But she kept trying for it.

"Elsa ..." Indy said, trying to keep his voice calm. "Give me your other hand, honey." Feeling her gloved hand begin to slip through his grasp, his voice grew louder with mounting panic as he said, "I can't hold you!"

"I can reach it," Elsa said, keeping her eyes obsessively fixed on the Grail. "I can reach it."

Her right hand slid slightly out of her glove. Indy clamped his fingers even more tightly around hers, but he could feel he was losing her.

"Elsa, give me your hand. Give me your other hand!"

But Elsa kept her left hand extended toward the Grail. And then her right hand slipped again.

"Elsa!"

She screamed as she plummeted into the chasm, falling past the jagged walls of rock to her death far below. Before Indy could pull himself back, the stone that he lay upon crumbled and broke apart. He threw his arms out as he tumbled over the edge, just as Henry moved fast to grab Indy's right hand.

Indy found himself in the same position that Elsa had been. He looked to his left and saw the Grail on the ledge.

"Junior, give me your other hand," Henry said. "I can't hold on!"

"I can get it," Indy said in a harsh whisper. He stretched out his left arm as far as he could. "I can almost reach it, Dad." One of his fingers actually brushed against the side of the Grail.

"Indiana . . ." Henry said, keeping his voice calm, just as Indy had done when he had tried to lure Elsa away from the Grail. "Indiana . . ."

Indy had never heard his father call him "Indiana"

before. His left arm went slack against his side, and he turned his head to look up into his father's eyes. Henry said, "Let it go."

Indy realized his father was straining at the effort to hang onto him. And although his father hadn't said it in so many words, he realized that his father cared more about him than he did for the Holy Grail.

Indy threw his left arm up to his father. Henry grabbed it and hauled Indy up over the edge. Sallah and Brody had been braced against a nearby wall, and now that Indy and Henry were all right, they edged toward the exit. As the ground went on rumbling and rocks continued to fall, Henry was about to head for a way out when he saw a shadowy figure looming at the top of the stairway between the lion statues. The figure was the Grail's ages-old guardian.

The knight gazed through the falling debris to Henry.

More stones began to fall, and Indy rushed to Brody and Sallah, steering them toward safety. Then Indy saw that his father had stopped walking and was staring back at the upper passage. "Dad . . ." Indy said, and then followed his father's gaze to see the knight.

The knight raised his right arm, saluting Henry across the temple chamber.

"Please, Dad," Indy said.

Henry looked at the knight for just a moment longer

before he turned and ran with Indy. They didn't look back at the knight, who continued to stand there with his hand raised, watching the men run away. As Indy and Henry hurtled out of the temple, a stone column crashed down behind them, sealing off the temple and leaving the knight to his fate.

EPILOGUE

*I*ndy and Henry bolted down the steps outside the ancient, palatial entrance to the temple. From behind, they heard the roar of walls caving in, and a high cloud of dust rolled out from the large, rectangular doorway and then crashed like a wave onto the ground outside. Ahead of them, they saw Sallah and Brody had already reached the horses that they'd left outside. There was no sign of the surviving soldiers.

When they reached a safe distance from the temple's entrance, Indy stopped and turned to face it. The rumbling had ceased, and the dust appeared to be settling. Indy gazed at the temple's façade and thought of Elsa.

He really had cared for her.

Henry looked at Indy, then walked up beside him and said, "Elsa never really believed in the Grail. She thought she'd found a prize."

Turning to face his father, Indy said, "What did *you* find, Dad?"

"Me?" Henry said. His eyes flicked to the façade and back to Indy as he mulled over the question, and then he answered, "Illumination."

Sallah and Brody had already mounted their horses. As Henry and Indy climbed onto their own, Henry looked to his son and said, "And what did you find, Junior?"

"'*Junior*?'" Indy snapped. "Dad . . ." He raised his hand and aimed an accusatory finger at his father.

"Please," Sallah interrupted, looking at Indy. "What does it always mean, this . . . this 'Junior?'"

"That's his name," Henry informed Sallah. "Henry Jones, Junior."

"I *like* Indiana," Indy muttered as he averted his gaze to the sandstone wall in front of him.

Leaning out from his saddle to scowl at his son, Henry said, "We named the *dog* Indiana."

Brody interrupted, "May we go home now, please?"

Sallah stared at Indy and bellowed, "The *dog*?!" Sallah chuckled. "You are named after the dog?" And then Sallah roared with laughter.

Keeping his eyes on the sandstone, Indy said, "I've got a lot of fond memories of that dog." Then he turned his head to face his father and Sallah, as if daring them to challenge him on the subject. While Sallah continued to laugh, Henry removed a handkerchief from his pocket, draped it over his head, and then wrapped and tied his bowtie around his head to fashion an improvised *keffiyeh.* When his father was done tying off the bowtie, Indy said, "Ready?"

"Ready," Henry replied.

"Indy! Henry!" Brody exclaimed. "Follow me! I know the way!" To his horse, he cried out, "Haaa!"

Brody had a tight grip on the reigns, but he nearly fell off his horse's back as it launched off into the narrow gorge that led back to the high desert. From their own horses, Sallah, Henry, and Indy watched Brody's departure with some amusement.

Turning to his son, Henry said, "Got lost in his own museum, huh?"

"Uh-huh," Indy said.

Henry gestured toward the gorge and said, "After you, Junior."

"Yes, sir," Indy said. He jerked his horse's reigns and shouted, "Haaa!"

Indy rode off after Brody. Sallah and Henry followed. They rode at full gallop, weaving through and out of the Canyon of the Crescent Moon. It wasn't until they exited the canyon and arrived at the edge of the wide-open desert plain that Indy finally caught up with Brody and helped the man right himself on his horse.

The four men rode off, heading off across the desert toward the setting sun. Indy cast one last glance back toward the Canyon of the Crescent Moon. This might have been his grandest adventure yet, but he was sure it wouldn't be his last.